JON GOWER has over thirty books to his name, in Welsh and English, including *The Story of Wales* which accompanied the landmark BBC series, *An Island Called Smith* which gained the John Morgan Travel Writing Award, and *Y Storïwr* which won the Wales Book of the Year award. He is a former BBC Wales arts and media correspondent and was for many years the presenter of Radio Wales' arts' programme *First Hand*. He lives in Cardiff with his wife Sarah and daughters Elena and Onwy. His next book will be a portrait of Benji Webbe, lead vocalist for the heavy metal band Skindred.

OWEN MARTELL writes novels and short stories in English and in Welsh. His most recent novel, *Intermission*, was an Irish Times Book of the Year in 2013.

S MARK GUBB is a visual artist based in Cardiff, where he lives with his wife, Sally, and daughter, Isabella. He grew up in Herne Bay, Kent, and, having failed to become a rock star, moved to Derby in the mid-90s to study art. His work has been exhibited widely, nationally and internationally, and includes several permanent public works around the UK.

Also by Jon Gower

Short Stories
Creep
Rebel, Rebel
Big Fish
Too Cold for Snow
Breision
Clymau (ed.)

Novels
Norte
Uncharted
Y Storiwr
Dala'r Llanw
Y Duwch

Travel
Wales: At Water's Edge
An Island Called Smith
Gwalia Patagonia

Essays
Homeland (ed.)
Arwyr Cymru
Teithio Drwy Hanes
Wales: In Our Own Image
A Year in a Small Country (ed.)

History
The Story of Wales
A Long Mile
Real Llanelli
Peace in the City

Young Adult
Academi Mr Dŵm

Biography
Encounters with Nigel Jenkins (ed.)
Vigilant Imagination: Encounters with John Selway
Encounters with Karl Francis
Encounters with Dylan Thomas (ed.)

Translation
My Life in History by John Davies

The
Murenger
and
Other Stories

by
Jon Gower

Foreword by
Owen Martell

Photographs by
S Mark Gubb

Three Impostors
3 Woodville Road,
Newport,
South Wales,
NP20 4JB

www.threeimpostors.co.uk

First published in 2019

Printed and bound by Y Lolfa,
Talybont, Ceredigion, SY24 5HE

ISBN 978-1-78461-812-4

Contents

Foreword

I encountered at least a few of the stories before meeting the storyteller himself. I was just starting out, as they say – he was already up and running hard.

The first text was a radio document, prepared for the BBC's Millennium Oral History project. He had located and interviewed a Rhondda man, Brenig Jones, who, from his prisoner of war camp, had seen the mushroom cloud being unleashed, in unreal time, over Hiroshima. I, for my part, seeing the soundwaves of shock on a computer screen in Llandaf, intoned interconnections.

The other story from that time was one I would come to think of as 'vintage Jon'. I was sitting in on the recording of his interview for *Beti a'i phobl*, listening to him recount the loss of his first wife's wedding ring – on the first day of their honeymoon, no less – and the ensuing matrimonial chaos (of which there was a fair amount). It was beautifully told – bathetic and balletic, so to speak, in equal measure – and an ideal primer for the person I'd meet soon after.

I mention both these stories specifically because they could be said to exemplify not so much the *modus operandi* as the *modus vivendi* of the man. Jon – should I say 'Gower' to at least feign objectivity? – is a great producer and director of stories, and his latest crop, his 'Jon at 60' volume (though I would no more think to give him 60 years than I would to give the Río de la Plata, one of his rivers, sixty million), abounds here in purple plenty. But '*modus vivendi*' isn't quite right either, as it might also imply a pretence, even a certain guile in this most guileless of writers, this most guileless of men. For as gifted as he is in the telling of his own stories, he is just as good at nurturing, encouraging and inviting others to tell theirs, on radio and on paper. He is also, I would venture to say, pretty much peerless in his enjoyment, his appreciation, and his optimism for what writing – and reading – are and can be, as acts of humanity. He revels in the phrases of others every bit as much as he does in his own (much more so, in fact, because in that respect he is modest too). But it isn't just writing – it is music and art, history, natural history and geography, geology, anthropology, sociology... He is the sensitive soul, the reader turned writer *par excellence*, and those influences, those thrills felt, pepper his texts compulsively. The most compassionate of companions: he's heard something good and he can't bear not to share it with you... What's more, it'll be accompanied by the meanest margarita this side of the Mariana trench.

Paradoxically, though, I think that this extreme generosity has also led to a certain misapprehension, or misappreciation, with regard to his fiction at least. *The Cambridge History of Welsh Literature* calls that work a 'heady combination of fantasy, travel and touches of postmodernism', which is fair enough as a summary description, having the virtue too of not being inaccurate. But it isn't sufficient either.

Because, in my opinion, a characterisation as 'teller of tales' or 'spinner of yarns' masks the deeper purpose at work in Jon's fiction and non-fiction alike, and which is a direct consequence of his generosity, and of writing – and reading – as acts of humanity.

That deeper purpose is particularly visible, I think, in one of the most prominent aspects of his writing which I will characterise, because I can, as a sort of animistic onomatology. But what I mean by that is actually perfectly simple – and wonderfully complex: it is the seemingly pathological inability to let things go unnamed or untold. In the stories that follow, 15 of them as well as 15,000 more, Jon combines the name-giving of the *cyfarwydd* in medieval Welsh tradition with an exuberant – and endearingly Victorianate – encyclopaedism (which is almost diametrically opposed to the JFGI ethos of our time) and the awed reverence of the pilgrim passing through. Sometimes he brings news from afar, at others he reminds and rejigs, from traditions and know-how closer to home but no longer in our common access. Either way, a bird cannot be a bird if it is, in fact, Steller's sea eagle or jay, a tanning bed in a Caerphilly girl's ambition is never just a lot of metal and wires, and a pub in Newport is avowedly not a pub if it also happens to contain a whole Murenger's-worth of stories...

And all of that, less literary trope than a basic condition of the man, the writer's being, is gloriously, non-cynically human, humane – and more: writing as we must do henceforth from the Anthropocene, and impending catastrophe that demands that we listen to the so-called 'natural world' as never before, all the elements in Jon's natural world demand to be heard; the agency of birds, rivers, rocks, a wild inferno even, seeks equality with that of the human protagonists. And it is in this sense, I think, that 'the story's the thing' in his work. In order to tell them, you have to know them – and vice versa, of course. Which leads us back to the storyteller himself, and to the reason why I started this piece by mentioning two of his stories – one personal, the other one which became him. I see now that I recognised the tale of his disastrous first marriage (though I'll always thank goodness that it was disastrous or I would never have met Sarah, Elena and Onwy), as 'vintage Jon' not because he was some genial raconteur of deliberately self-deprecating ego but because he was, and is, the exact opposite of that. Many of the stories in this collection are exceedingly personal, as is a great deal of his work – yet he avoids the I of exposition not like the proverbial but like the plague of Justinian, in Byzantium, which was the first recorded outbreak of bubonic plague, between 541 and 750 (you see? you *can't* just turn it on for effect...). And I will hazard a guess too as to why that is: it is because he knows, as sure as eggs is eggs, that the best way to tell your own story is to tell someone else's. Even when you're the main character. He knows, I think, in magnanimity, that the catharsis of writing, and the humanity of reading, lie less in seeing one's innermost soul laid out on a page in terrible, circumstantial detail than in feeling the pulse, rather, on a plane with all the other souls, all the other stories – human, animal, geological – singing across the songlines.

Owen Martell, 2019

Skin Hue

Steph's friends had their various dreams of deep romance and wild adventure but she had just the one. And it had come true. As soon as she opened the door to Steph's Sunshine World it was as if she was strolling onto the Elysian fields. Flicking the light switches was enough to make her tremble. Hers. Her place. Her dream.

It was the little touches that did it. The fresh gladioli, a spray of traffic light red, arranged by her Auntie Lil who had a good eye for colour. Then there was the background music, hand picked by her husband Sean from across a wide sea of genres – jazz saxophone by Ben Webster blending into ambient noodling by Brian Eno. No other tanning place had music as relaxing as this. You could fall asleep standing up.

Steph switched on the half dozen tanning machines, the best on the market. She had done her research thoroughly. The Solarity 400 came with a whole online galaxy of five star reviews and had been available at zero interest. Warming up, the Solarities hummed, a quietly zizzing choir of miniaturized insects. Steph switched on the till before stepping through into the small kitchen where Sean had installed a gift of an espresso maker. She loved him with all her heart.

One of the most intriguing documents that had accompanied the machines was the colour chart showing the possible tans, described in ridiculous language, like those catalogues of posh paint which listed 'Mole's Breath,' 'Mizzle,' 'Worsted,' 'Lamp Room Grey.' The shiny leaflet claimed one could 'solarize into a range of skin hues and dermal deepening' such as – and here Steph had to laugh – 'Bermuda Blush,' 'Old Church Door' and the unequivocal 'Deep Teak.' There was even one called 'Plywood' which was marketed much like perfume as its full name was 'Plywood by Guy Savant.' For the woman who wanted her skin to resemble an IKEA kitchen chair, thought Steph. Plywood, for fuck's sake.

The grand opening was at eleven so she had to busy herself, quickly blowing up balloons and giving every surface a final, shining wipe. With a silvery tinkling of the front door bell Sunshine Land would be officially open. Forty nine people had accepted her invitation for a celebratory glass of Prosecco, and a chance to benefit from a six-for-three deal on hourly sessions.

There was one snag. An altercation over a parking space meant that Steph had fallen out with her neighbour, Steve, who was, by reputation, a witch. The falling out had been swift, Steve spitting out a splenetic curse. He had the voice for it, worked as a bingo caller who in his spare time studied very dark arts. Envenomed by anger at the fact that her car was parked in his spot Steve spat out words like a spitting cobra lining up a scampering mouse.

'The black clouds will rain poison down upon you, and your loved ones blind will be.'

There he was, Steve from Gala Bingo, in the twenty first century, drawing down rain clouds of doom, on the other side of the garden fence.

Steph had wanted to ask him to be reasonable, to take it all back but he had stormed off into the house, slamming the door so hard that the very mantle of the earth shook and tsunami waves were shocked into being oceans away. Steve had the powers, of that there was no doubt, sure as two fat ladies.

Little wonder that Steph's enjoyment of the opening was sullied by the nagging of the curse. Sean had even been around to see the guy but his only response had been to empty a chamber pot of piss over his head as he stood at the front door.

'Mad, that one,' he had sputtered before taking another shower.

They started to arrive at ten to eleven, women dressed in bright colours and chattering like parakeets. Her husband stood sentinel at the Prosecco table, beaming and doing that thing he did so well, namely strike up animated conversation with a total stranger at the flick of a switch. There was a tremulousness in Steph's voice as she delivered her prepared speech.

'Thank you for coming to share my dream. I know that many of you think it's a weird thing to want in life, a tanning parlour, but ever since my first session in The Goldening Room, you remember the place, down off Clifton Street, I thought this was the best thing ever. We hope you'll sign up for some sessions. Our special tanning machines offer a choice of tones, from honeydew through Jamaican bikini to rich mahogany. Out back we have six artifical suns, all available by the hour for as little as £6.99.'

The gathering laughed at the mix of lyrical and commercial even as Auntie Lil stepped up to the mike to offer her sincere congratulations and suggest that she was going to turn herself into a honey brown sex bomb over the course of the next six weeks.

'Men of Caerphilly, watch out,' she concluded, with a delicious wiggle of her new hip.

They signed up 31 new customers and during the afternoon there was a steady trickle of enquiries, including one lovely old man who wondered whether the treatments were any good for common or garden aches and pains. Steph offered him a free trial but he explained that he'd need help taking off his clothes as one of his arms didn't work as well as it used to. So Steph helped him disrobe and even went out to Greggs to get a cup of soup when he said he didn't drink tea or coffee.

The final visitor of the day was a wary Jamaican man who behaved as if he expected her to to suggest he was already tanned enough, but when she took his money with a smile he volunteered the fact that he suffered from seasonal affective disorder. He told her about a morning when he'd gone to a nudist beach in Pendine on a February morning to find that he was one of three Caribbeans 'shivering their nuts off' as he put it. 'We crave God's lamp in the cold of winter. The thing is...' he went on, '... Skin is skin. It's not a badge of difference. It's wrapped around all humans. You are my sister. Your skin connects you to me. Melanin is a pigment we all share.'

Steph gave him a family discount and a loyalty card to boot. He made her feel warm inside, connected.

At day's end the takings were £148 which wasn't that great considering the outgoings. They had also signed up a lot of people on the six session plan so there would be lots more money flowing in. But that, and the smiles on the old man's face were not enough to dispel the anxiety that fluttered in Steph's stomach, a lepidoptera of fear. It was the witch's curse, settling deep inside her.

Things didn't improve the next morning. Being a Sunday, there was a meeting of the book club and they were reading Chinua Achebe's *Things Fall Apart* which was exactly how she felt, falling apart at the thought of the future and its dissolutions. Bet, who chaired the meeting was a gloomy soul. You could depend on her to kickstart the meeting with some grim news.

'Did you hear about the woman who's suing a tanning place in Rochester because they forgot about her and she ended up with second degree burns. All over. Her skin looked like a meringue. I hope that sort of thing never happens to you Steph. But it's a cautionary tale, sure as eggs is eggs.'

Steph was usually immune to Bet's barbs but today they hooked. She could easily have cried a river but managed to locate some inner steel to staunch the flow.

The group animatedly talked about the book, with most of them agreeing they loved Okonkwo the wrestler while also being chastened by the dire things Europeans had done in Africa. They then drifted seamlessly into chit chat and scandal-spreading, with some really juicy and salacious gobbets available to them after Hilda's divorce from the man they referred to as Desperate Dan. Steph wasn't really listening so when her name was mentioned she was a tad startled.

'I hear that bingo witch been giving you some gyp,' repeated Marta, prowling the dirt as usual.

'He's been a bit forthright in his cursing, to say the least.'

'The vicar's got his number, mind. He can exorcise the bad spirits, banish the ju-ju if you want. He did exactly this when Steve fell out with Hetty and planted such a deadly bee in her bonnet that all her hair fell out. Raging alopecia it was. Bald for weeks.'

'Which vicar? The one at St Michael's?' asked Steph, cautiously cheering up at the news.

'Expert on poltergeists apparently. Travels the country.'

Terry was first in on Monday and while Steph helped him prepare for the lamp he teased her with vigour.

'I'll be like a Greek god by the time you've finished with me...'

'Without a doubt.'

'Which one?'

'Apollo, he'd be appropriate for this place...'

The name drew a blank.

'God of the sun. And music. He's a good one.'

'Good how?'

'He had power over light.'

Terry asked for just a half hour session, enough to warm his bones down to the marrow and suggested that Steph should consider discounts for OAPs like the one they did on fish and chips down The

Codfather. She thought it was such a good idea she asked Terry to model for a poster. They would do so on Wednesday after session number three when he would look like the man who had been to Magaluf. A god come to live among them.

The other customers that day included a dodgy drug dealer who wanted a skintone to match the vulgarity of the bling that covered his torso like a Pharoah.

After work Steph phoned the vicarage and arranged to visit the Reverend Lionel Speedwell, the following day at six.

She never made that meeting.

As she rode to work the next morning Steph could hear Steve's bitter, mantric words repeating as if on a tape loop. 'The black clouds... Your loved ones blind.' Steph had even thought about leaving her husband just to keep him safe, such was the raw and twisted power of the man's malediction. And Sean's eyes were his best feature.

Edgy. Everything was edge that morning. The timer on the espresso machine was irritating as a mosquito whine. Terry annoyed her simply by making a mark on one of the newly painted walls when he dropped his stick. She snapped at him before drowning in a wave of regret. Such a nice old man.

She checked the machines carefully, using the manual. Steph had heard about a man who had ended up completely two tone because he'd forgotten to turn around during a tanning session and so had a tangerine front and a back the colour of Mother's Pride bread.

She set Terry's timer going and then showed a new customer the ropes, suggesting she could have a lanolin scrub at the end, or even try the new oxygen bar which Steph assured her was all the rage. 'Relax. Refresh. Rejuvenate,' as the logo had it. They had bayberry, cranberry and wintergreen flavoured gas, which customers sucked up through plastic pipes unattractively known as cannulas. The woman was an interesting sort, full of jokes and earthy wisdom and

Steph lost sight of the time rather.

Then came the bang, as cubicle number four supernovaed, as if a small sun had well and truly exploded. By the time Steph reached Terry he was frantically running his fingers across his eyes as if he was trying to coax them back into seeing. As she cradled his head she heard an agonised squeal from the new customer, whose body hair had started to singe. Both phones went off simultaneously even as she smelled a different kind of burning. She was just in time to see the Solarity 400 in Room 3 seem to self ignite and, to add to her woes, the fire extinguisher turned out to be empty.

'My pubes are on fire,' yelled the woman.

'What's going on?' shouted Terry, abandoned in his darkness.

'It's just an eclipse,' said Steph, trying to act calm. 'It'll all pass. It's just a small shift in the universe, things slipping in and out of alignment. Nothing to worry about.'

But the blinded man and the singed woman and the hollow extinguisher spoke eloquently otherwise. This was an incident too awful for phlegmatism. This was a jinx, a pre-determined doom, the witch's curse coming true.

For Terry's world had been condemned to darkness.

A woman's private parts had been set on fire and she would definitely sue.

Two of the machines were fire damaged beyond repair.

In the elms outside the vicarage a raucous crew of jackdaws croaked like witches before lifting, chattering briskly into to the sky, like black rags of paper rising up above a bonfire, climbing up to pixillate the sun.

Short Stay

The brothers were skirting the foothills, where the road curves through low juniper when they heard the whoosh of rockets. They hit the brakes, skidding in a skittering shower of gravel before hurling themselves off the bikes.

They both tumbled hard before coming to a bolt-jolting stop, yards only from each other. Lee looked at his brother calmly checking his limbs for fractures and had to laugh.

'Another great holiday, Al.'

'Best yet,' he agreed, proudly showing the huge tear in one leg of his leathers. Underneath there was a lot of scarlet blood.

His brother remembered something Al had written about him once, 'I would go through storms for this man.' And they had been through a few, deepening their bonds all the while. Two divorces, one a mathematical definition of foolhardiness, with the financial settlement off the graph and the other a bitter essay about deceit. One illness, that gusted through Lee's insides like a gale trying to dislodge his soul. And one falling out between the two of them, that had seemed terminal until Al made a late night call and they met up to polish off a bottle of Woodford's Reserve together. Which led to their first dangerous holiday together in the Crimea. Which in turn had led to this grim situation...

'What now?'

The answer came as the sound of more incoming munitions,

throwing up great sprays of earth and filling the air with a vivid scent of blasted cedar and napalmed sage.

'Keep down and we'll stay intact. It's just a passing mortar attack.'

Both brothers smiled, even though they were under fire, in a strange country, with their motorbikes totally un-roadworthy, with the front forks of one twisted to buggery and the other one leaking petrol from the tank. Lee, the mechanic and pragmatist, could perform rudimentary roadside fixes but this was a machine-shop job and they were far, far from anything like that. This was the Golan Heights after all, and they weren't meant to be here in the first place. Strictly, strictly so.

But that was the point of the holiday. To go to places other people simply do not go. The challenge was in the getting there, and then staying there, and finally in simply keeping alive when danger swirled all around. Al loved the romance of danger, the exacting lure of the forbidden. He also loved his brother in a way that went beyond normal bounds. 'I would go through storms for this man.' It had much to do with the fact that one was adopted and one was not. The bonds between were strong – unbreakable as high tensile steel.

That morning they had visited a cave system which ranked as major tourist attraction here in the Golan, the entrance guarded by a lone Israeli soldier, 24/7, 365 days-a-year, to make sure the tunnels couldn't be used for weapon smuggling. Lee and Al enjoyed being here simply because so few people ever managed to. They demonstrated the strength of their brotherly links by putting themselves in danger and looking after each other when the shit hit. When they were questioned by an intelligence officer at the cave entryway Al showed him his sketch book of local butterflies – detailed studies of painted ladies, leopard butterflies and Turkish meadow browns – which seemed to satisfy the man. That and the three permits and the letter of introduction from Al's university.

Once the shelling had finally stopped Lee asked his brother if he was in good enough shape to get the hell out of there. Al replied by getting to his feet, firing up his Zippo lighter and tossing it at his Kawasaki which turned fireball in seconds.

'Guess I won't be needing the steed any longer,' Al mumbled in his best Marlon Brando.

'That's like telling the soldiers exactly where we are,' Lee observed, as smoke started to spiral high into the azure.

'Which is why we need to hightail it out of here.'

'Cross country running? In motorcycle boots?' said a bemused Lee.

'Three, two, one, go...'

Al started loping away and his brother followed, his breathing a-stutter as if something had happened to a rib as he came off the bike. But soon they were in their stride, running as one, keeping their heads down even as they picked up speed. There was precious little cover, so they were awkward as armadillos as they crossed the terrain. In the distance they saw sunlight flare off the windows of a Land Rover which sped along, sending up plumes of dust. It seemed to be travelling in parallel with them.

The brothers kept on running, their breath in their hands, when they saw the building and had to stop. It was a house, painted white and brilliantly luminiscent this high noon. It was the sign that did it, though. 'Crazy Nate's Guest House.' And underneath a small letterbox of a sign saying 'Vacancies.'

'Crazy's the word,' said Lee.

'Let's see what the rooms are like.'

'You're kidding right?'

'Listen, what I need right now is to freshen up before lunch and try to forget the monumental fucking catastophe of a situation that is gathering around us. Anyway, look at the walls.'

'What of it? They're white.'

'And not pockmarked by bulletholes of any kind. Let's go in.'

The tiny reception lobby was made even smaller by the man sitting in a Rattan chair. He had girth issues: even the braces on his trousers were stretched taut by the sheer, overwhelming bulk of the man.

'Room gentlemen? One or two?' he panted, getting up on hydraulic legs.

'One will be fine? We're brothers.'

'Where's the accent from?'

'Llansamlet... in Wales.'

'Ah yes. Gareth Bale's country.'

The brothers acted as if they hadn't heard this a dozen times these past three weeks. A man in Jerusalem had even displayed a tattoo of the football player on his wrist.

'Got any ID? Oh don't worry. If that lot over there come here we'll say you're with the UN and if that lot over there come here we'll tell them you're press. That work?'

'Do they come here a lot?'

'Hardly ever, 'said the man, swabbing sweat off of his brow with a big kitchen sponge. 'I think they all find it amusing that I've got this place up and running in a war zone.'

'How do you get the staff?

'One man band pretty much. I've got a boy who helps, but he lives down below the trees and comes up when he feels like it or when he can. So, among other things I'm the cook, that is when there's any food. We go from shortage to famine and back again on a weekly basis. No loaves, no fishes and so it's a bloody miracle I'm the size I am.'

Lee imagined him in the kitchen, managing to braise vegetables in his own sweat. Wherever he was in the little galley space inevitably a part of him was under the grill. He was that big: he cut a Zeppelin figure.

'I'll get Noah to show you to your room. We can faff with the paper later.'

Nate rang a little silver bell and a boy swung in with the agility of a gibbon, and took both their pannier bags with him as he jumped the stairs three at a time.

The room was big enough for two adults as long as they were pre-shrunk.

'Great, we'll take it,' said Luke, taking in the view from the small monastery-style window. They could see the clumped radio masts flowering like metal daisy heads and long lines of razor wire, strung across the landscape as a weird festive decoration. It had an appealing desolation to it, as landscapes go. A picture postcard scene, if the sender was a psycho.

In the morning the brothers were woken by sniper fire, then a cock crowing and then a clipped gurgling sound which might have been the bird being taken out by the self-same sniper.

In the small dining area Nate was dressed the part of mein host, with a Noël Coward style necktie and a smoking jacket with velvet trim.

'Gentlemen, gentlemen, may I officially welcome you to your first full day at Nate's. You'll be pleased to know we have three kinds of fresh juice. Orange, pomegranate and persimmon. Or what I suggest is a mix of all three. Oh it is such a life affirming cocktail. We may not have much but what we have is heavenly.'

One of the other guests made an appearance and what an appearance. He looked like a cross between a God-crazed hermit and an Interpol 'Wanted' poster.

'Let me introduce The Chechnyan. No need to know his real name because if you did learn it he'd have to garotte you with his bare hands. He's in the room next door to you so you should feel safer there than anywhere else in the building. If there's trouble, he's your go-to-guy.'

The wild-haired man bowed his head, shaking loose some mud-clagged dreadlocks and muttering a lupine growl before holding out a hand stained mahogany by the weather.

'He doesn't do small talk I'm afraid and if he did start telling us about his life it would no doubt sound like a catalogue of the ills of the twenty first century. He has been a mercenary on four continents and he has left mangled cars, exploded bodies and eighteen kinds of hell in his wake.'

'If this man is as dangerous as you say he is, how come he is free to roam in this, one of the most dangerous and well, fenced-off zones in the world?' asked Lee, forever in search of the rational in the irrational mayhem.

The Chechnyan looked at the three of them, as if he too was eager to hear the answer.

'Go-between. He's the ultimate envoy between one proscribed organisation and another. And he has the keys to the new toys, gets to play with CIA try-out weaponry in real battlefield situations or gets sent Thermos flasks of biochemical attack-grade viruses and what not.'

'So best not to take up any invitation to tea then...' suggested Al, wrily.

Nate looked a tad confused until Al repeated the word 'Thermos" which set the fat innkeeper off, laughing like a drain.

Composing himself, he encouraged them to sit down while he cooked them eggs on a griddle set up near the window.

Nate announced 'I come from the First Thermonuclear Strike School of Cooking,' turning up the gas jets so that they hissed like spitting cobras. 'Three eggs each be enough?' There wasn't time for a reply as something hit the hillside behind the B&B, making the huge rock shake as if the explosion was sufficient to sunder the very earth, shake it down to the mantle.

'Incoming,' yelled Nate, his body jellying downwards.

Three of them hit the floor at the same time, as the window glass blew in like a diamond shower.

Nate counted to ten before asking for a hand up.

'Close one. It's been getting increasingly busy around here. There used to be a pact that we were left alone, but I think that outside events are making everyone a bit jittery. They blew up the henhouse yesterday which is why these eggs are such precious orbs.' He went back to his whisk.

While he had been explaining this The Chechnyan, who had sat calmly at the table despite the explosion, was stripping down a semi-automatic rifle with the dexterity of a surgeon, fitting part into part with an automaton certainty. He might have been the man who wrote the service manual (in Chechnyan, of course) . He grunted with satisfaction when he checked his watch and found he had reassembled the gun in record time, then stalked out, announcing that he would shoot a sandgrouse for supper.

Nate noticed the flame had gone out on his gas burner and looked around for a lighter but couldn't find one. Lee offered to look for it and Nate suggested that it was probably in The Chechnyan's room as he was forever borrowing it and forgetting to return it.

'Will he mind?'

Nate shook his head and Lee went to the door of Room Two. He was only gone for a matter of seconds before he returned, his face rigid with disquiet.

'What's wrong?' asked Al. 'Did you find the lighter?'

'I didn't find it,' Lee replied, his lower lip aquiver. 'On the other hand I did find an Israeli soldier strapped to a chair with his mouth covered in duct tape.'

'Not the one from the cave?'

' The very one. Gagged and bound.'

'Jesus,' said Nate. 'I knew the fucker'd do something stupid one day.'

'What shall we do?' asked Lee, his voice more than a little tremulous.

'I really don't know,' Nate answered, even as a new noise entered the kitchen. Outside a military drone was dropping leaflets.

'Postman's arrived,' said Nate, taking off his apron.

He stepped outside and picked up one of the mustard yellow pieces of paper.

It announced – starkly and in five languages – that they should evacuate the area first thing in the morning. It also announced a reward for the missing soldier, money equivalent to a king's ransom.

The three of them stood there, the brothers computing their share of the grand sum. Enough to buy two five bedroom houses back in Pontypool. With long back gardens.

'He'll be back soon. So if there was was a time to set a soldier free from his bonds then this is it.'

The trio seemed to be paralysed by the immensity of the decision, which hung over them with the weight of Jupiter.

The drone drew away, making a hornet whine which seemed an apposite soundtrack to the tense event unfolding at the breakfast table.

'He will fucking kill us,' ventured Lee.

'Unless the soldier's mates up in High Command order us killed first.'

'Rock and a hard place, brother.'

'Got any dice?'

Wordlessly the three of them walked to the bedroom door, as if summoned there by genies.

The soldier's eyeballs were out on stalks, a young man cacking himself despite his intensive IDF training.

Nate made the first move, stripping off the black tape from his mouth.

'I will untie you but you can't go outside. Outside there's a man with a gun who will kill you without blinking. Do you understand?'

The soldier nodded. Nate cut his bonds with the bread knife in his Cumberland sausage fingers. The crew then went into the sitting room to discuss what to do about the man in Room 2. Nate usefully went to get his own gun and cradled it on his lap as he led the discussion.

'If we can disarm him we'll be OK,' he suggested.

'And what do we do with him, tie him up instead of whatsisface here.'

'I am Lieutenant Gideon Grossman of the Israeli Defence Force. My serial number is 1578342.'

The waver in his voice was somehow transfixing.

'I can call off the air strike.'

'Which airstrike?'

'The one scheduled for ten in the morning.'

'Jesus,' said Nate. 'I thought they usually gave a bit more notice for Judgement Day. A bit of angel trumpeting first.'

Outside the tangerine sun was drifting down through a goldening haze. Lee looked at his watch and saw it was ten past six. The Chechnyan was breaking the six o'clock curfew on top of everything else.

'He's out there and if he moves then the guys with night sights and infra red will locate him and shoot him dead,' Nate informed them. 'That's the price we have to pay for staying open. If one of their missiles hits you you're liquidized into dog food. There's this big flash and a loud noise and then that's that.'

'So tell me again. How do you manage to stay open?' Lee enquired.

'People just can't believe anyone would be mad enough to run a bed and breakfast in a disputed territory and militarized zone. They let me stay here for nothing more explainable than bemusement. Respect for an ornery character. My late wife often used to ask who on earth was crazy enough to sell ice cream at the North Pole? And this is my answer. Creating this five star hotel smack bang in the middle of a war zone. It's my memorial to her for I loved her madly.'

'Dare I ask why you're here?' said Nate.

No time for an answer. The evening air was rent by the tat-tat-tat of gunfire but Nate didn't know enough about weapons to identify the sound of the different bullet sprays. It sounded close. Had The Chechnyan met his end or was he now the happy hunter?

Nate calmed himself by looking in the fridge. 'The fucker's taken the last of the pomegranate juice,' he said, pointing out the empty shelves. 'I guess there won't be any breakfast.'

Meanwhile Lee took stock. They were in a bed and breakfast where there was   nothing for breakfast and a Chechnyan mercenary was possibly on the loose outside if he wasn't lying dead. There had been an airdrop of messages warning them to skedaddle by morning when they would most likely be smithereened by heavy armour. And they had a hostage, an ashen faced Israeli soldier sipping the last of the mint tea at the table. As if this wasn't enough the local news had announced that Donald Trump had taken sides in the dispute over the Golan Heights and so the world was looking this way, not just the Syrian soldiers on one side and the Israelis on the other. It was now a patch of land as politicized as the Suez canal once was or the lawless forests of the Congo were today.

Down in the valley they could hear the rumbling of tanks, a drumming thrum of earthmoving vehicles that sounded big enough to move the Earth. Strange lime-coloured lights moved along the tracks. There was a dread sense of preparedness, the shrill zizz of cicadas outside seemingly amplified as if the insects quivered their song into a huge tin bucket, resonating metallically. In the enpurpled sky the moon rose as a cream balloon, washing the plateau outside with serene light, quite out of keeping with the heavy armour lumbering forward on great caterpillar tracks down in the valley.

'So what are we going to do?' Al asked of the assembled company. 'Do you think looney tunes is coming back with a necklace worth of scalps, or can we tick him off our growing list of concerns?'

The soldier offered his solution, being the caves and that with two options. They could get to the cave either by running – and thereby running the risk of being picked off by snipers with night vision sights – or they could crawl there, thereby lessening the chances of being spotted, but it would take them longer and it would feel as if it was taking much, much longer. Crawling for a frightened century.

'And when we get to the caves, what then?' asked Lee, injecting reality into the plan.

'I think there's a way through,' said the soldier. 'That's why they station us at the entrance. Someone knows this and wants to keep it a secret. I've been quite far as there's nothing else to do when you're up there.'

'So they'll follow us?'

'I can deal with that,' said Gideon, allowing a grim smile to appear. 'I can always blow up the entrance.'

'Nothing to lose then, 'said Nate, placing a glass in front of each of them and sharing the contents of a bottle of Schnapps between them, which meant filling each glass up to the brim.

'To the caves,' came the toast.

'To the caves,' came the reply as they drank the fiery drink.

'I'll be staying here,' announced Nate. 'This is my home and besides a fat man ain't no sprinter.'

There was a stunned communion of understanding: the sadness splintering in each and every heart. Nate called the boy and set him free, telling him to take the secret path down to his grandfather's house, assuring him he'd be safe there. Another glint of sadness, like an ice shard driven into the skin by an awl.

The rumbling in the valley was by now deep, throaty, sub-sonic. The crew gathered at the front door and, counted down by Nate, they ran as one, covering the ground faster than fast. Al and Lee connected with their younger selves, running through Stradey woods on the cross-country races at school. Al pumped his legs, fiercely aware that he hadn't run anywhere for nigh on thirty years but knew he needed to pretend he'd been training hard for some marathon or other and was in peak condition. While the Israeli – the Israeli soldier they were having to trust against all logic – was setting the pace, eating up the yards. And then they were there and the Gods had smiled on them because the high-ups hadn't got round to replacing Gideon yet, so they were able to edge into the dark cleft in the rock and disappear from the world.

The darkness was absolute and Gideon refrained from using his torch until they had gone further into the black bowels. When he switched it on they could see that there were some big halls of space and many crevices and gulleys where the stone was fractured, dislocated shards of rock pushing outwards like spears.

'This way,' announced Gideon, kicking himself that he hadn't thought of bringing more torches, as the light was insufficient, given the number of obstacles, the sharp sprigs of rock that snagged your feet. Hazards aplenty.

They walked for hours and by three in the morning the water had all gone and they were all wounded in some way. Overhangs bludgeoned foreheads, unicorn horns of stalactite ripped into calves and ankles. The trio stumbled forward, a spasticity in their movements by now, a sapping weariness acting like a drag of weights behind each one of them.

Al and Lee were holding hands as they advanced, and it was comforting as well as awkward to go down the increasingly narrow confines of the tunnel. Lee was whistling a defiant ditty, which he identified as a song by Tom Waits.

Things got darker and tighter and more oppressive and their trust in their guide wavered as they spiralled slowly down. And then they reached a rockfall and the path seemed blocked completely but Gideon lifted himself onto a little ledge and shone his torch to show them what they had to do.

The soldier disappeared into the innards of the planet, as one brother helped the other clamber up, both breathing stertorously as they pushed into the black hole.

The other side of the cramped opening was even tighter, claustrophobic to the nth degree. They squeezed like human toothpaste through cavesides that compressed with the grip of a boa constrictor, flattening rib cages, challenging each breath.

And then they saw it, a grey smudge of light seemingly daubed on a wall. There was even a pale hint of mandarin, indicative of sunrise.

'You are a mighty brother,' said Lee to Al, helping his brother clamber over a jagged floor of scree.

'I love you *brawd*.'

And as their eyes grew accustomed to the morning gloam, and the broadening horizon of the next stage of their grim adventure, the brothers couldn't stop themselves from laughing. Brotherhood had brought them here, or was it brothership? To this wild extreme of a situation, entering the Syrian side. Al thought of Nate in his guest house and hoped he'd be OK, when instinct told him otherwise. He had probably been incinerated in his own kitchen. Helicopters were strafing the hills as if they'd been ordered to get rid of ammunition. There was one huge explosion, as a daisy cutter bomb had gone off, the bang loud enough to wake the dead in Tel Aviv.

Meanwhile, Lee's mind ran through a Rolodex list of war zones. If they got through this alive they would have to do some planning. He would go anywhere, simply anywhere with his brother at his side. Join the Kurds near the Turkish border. Visit the Polisario-held areas of Western Sahara. Afghanistan, too, held its appeal and terrors in perfect balance. Help his brother look for butterflies in Helmand Province in the spring. There was some incredibly rare swallowtail apparently, high up in the mountains. They must start saving up.

The
Mind's Menagerie

He examined the rims of the ice cave as if they might connect in some way with the frozen chambers of his heart. George Steller has come a long way in a brief life, endured so many travails only for it to end here, in this complete desolation.

He had been with Bering on that great expedition, as the two ships, the Peter and the Paul set out *to discover*. And discover they did, from Alaskan mountains girt with the whitest snow that any of them had ever seen to the sharp teeth of the Aleutian Islands that were new to any map. In those glaucous and preternaturally perilous waters Bering took both ships through near un-navigable sea passes – Unimak, Umnak, Amukta, Seguam. Steller liked Bering, trusted his unfathomable skills and his habit of swearing loudly in his native Danish, words that burst out of him like firecrackers. Bering recognized that Steller was a fellow voyager and adventurer, and a little boy to boot, childishly eager to learn things, see things, give them names, to know their most intimate habits. In another world, another age they might have been lovers.

But Steller was now alone. Last man on earth alone at that. The ship was going to sink and leave no trace, of that he was certain. Most of the crew were already down with Davy Jones, feasting on barnacles and dark water kelp. Fool that he was, he should have known this was a crew that wished him not a farthing's worth of goodwill. He had a store of hurts from so many journeys but this last one was the worst, voyaging with malcontents, blaggards and scoundrels. This ship crewed itself with criminals, desperate men who should have been bound for Van Diemen's Land and the other prison colonies.

He should have known from that very first day, when he gang-planked his way on board ship.

'Name,' the man had barked at him.

'George Stellar. Ship's naturalist.'

'What the hell is one of those when it's at home... sir?'

'I work with the doctor.'

That usually shut them up, and it was largely true. He was often given both office space and billet with the onboard medical man. He'd had trouble with the last one mind, a raging alcoholic who had become so wild in his deliriums that he had downed all the formaldehyde from one of the sample jars and Steller had had to fashion an instant stomach pump from a pair of bellows and a length of surgical tube and thereby save the man's life, not to mention re-potting the bloated frog that had been in the jar. It had a mandarin coloured stripe running along its back. A beautiful creature in its way.

Which colour made him think of his wife Elspeth and how her hair flamed. Her red hair, splayed on the pillow, made ever more beautiful as she slept, or in repose.

Theirs was an easy marriage and he remembered how they were in bed, her careful abandon, the scent of violets and the honeycomb taste of her shoulders. They would have had children but her illness had come too soon, was too rapacious, a shadow that had started within her and had radiated outwards to cloud his sun. On the day of the funeral he had stood near the grave and seen the world as an empty Arctic wilderness, seen the diamond shards of pack ice drifting even though he was standing in the shadow of some yew trees in a graveyard on a day of pallid sun and weak birdsong. A prophesy of how his life would be. Here in the farthest north.

The cave was the only shelter for miles and as he hunched further into it he could feel the wind outside biting at the back of his coat as if it had teeth. It really was that savage, a wind with teeth, tearing at his clothes, eager for the marrow.

But it wasn't all grief and shadows, oh no. He had had some rare adventures and seen things that no mortal man had ever seen before, or at least Stellar had been the first to register them.

There had been nothing like the dugongs he had sighted on his last voyage, sea-cows, huge as can be, drifting like icebergs. They were so human, the males and females hugging and embracing as they mated. And when some of his wayward shipmates went after them on a clubbing spree, killing one of the bigger animals, the other animals hopelessly attacked the ropes and the men and their harpoons, keening deeply as they did so.

The others – McCaw and Ruggins and that lot – just saw ways to satisfy their bloodlust but he had seen something else entirely. Underwater, the mammals submarined with such a mesmerising elegance, twisting among the kelp as if they were as much dancing as moving forward. Little wonder some witnesses had seen them and claimed them as mermaids. Maybe these were the original sea-maidens of fable, and their story had simply evolved into something enduring, one that commandeered the imagination. They shoaled in his mind, their movement a slow slalom among the chill water weeds.

His yelling at the blood mad men was in vain. Their harpoons plunged into the water and either their lunatic skills were enormous or the animals were too plentiful because almost every stab hit its mark. Steller imagined desperate sounds of keening spearing up from the depths as the harpooners thrust in and in again into the reddening water, each stabbing action eliciting a harrowing reply.

The next day was an unexpected benediction. The men, wearied by their murderous exertions, stayed beneath decks so Steller had the feeling they were going to make landfall and the captain, wandering down from the bridge said he should keep it under his hat, even though Stellar didn't have one and even if he didn't know what he should keep there under it.

He spent the day dissecting one of the sea cows, trying to disinter some central mystery of its creation. He was so very careful as he peeled back layers, unfolded the major organs, trying to take notes with hands that were slathered in oil and the mammal's blubber.

They had made landfall but it wasn't the way they intended, hitting a big floe which made the hull judder and shudder. Javelins of ice punctured the wood with the ease of outsize needles darning canvas and a deadly few bored in under the waterline, so that soon the ship was listing to starboard and groaning as would a choleric sailor in his death throes. They had just enough time to launch one of the lifeboats. Steller was able to haul his tired body on board before the first wash of seawater swept over the deck, taking some able-bodied seamen into the chill claws of the waves.

So, the ship was gone and he was pretty sure the whole crew with it. He was probably the only survivor. If there was any point in surviving to be left stranded here, with the cold spearing into the very core of his being. The cave was only the feeblest excuse for shelter as this Arctic wind that sent cold wires to flense the skin of his face was the real thing, an Arctic wind, and Stellar knew it would be the death of him.

He started to pray and that for the first time in his now curtailed life. His medical knowledge suggested that death from cold was long and tortuous, the opposite of a bullet in the brain, or an assassin's wire around the neck.

'Dear Lord...' he incanted. That was the entire length of his prayer as he heard the spars of the ship splinter into matchwood before the vessel – the only thing capable of getting him out of here – sank finally into the glaucous maw of the sea.

Alone. The word seemed as huge as a rock, the letters hewn out of granite. The cold clawed at his clothes, the cold now a whip, a tearing whip. *Kyrie eleison*. Be merciful. Have mercy on me.

He hunched his shoulder and brought down his head to enter the left aorta of the cave. The shivering was now making his fingers sound like castanets, his chattering teeth like an angry baboon sounding a warning.

The cave was about the size of his misery, the feeling that he was leaving all he loved behind. He tried to think of his wife but he could not *constitute* her. He had a glimpse of an upper arm, clad in a sleeve made of her favoured sky-blue silk. He managed an eye, but not two eyes and despite willing the other to appear he could not. The brain was now itself a cave, full of shadows, lengthening ones.

A bear would chance upon his body. 'Gadzooks, a man, a veritable feast from the south,' he would say to himself, before starting. His great teeth would chew down to the very marrow, turn his bones into meal and then into dust, an edible flour. And if the lumbering creature found him soon enough, or if the preservative effect of this place was as strong as science suggested, then the creature could dine on his innards too, grind them up slurpily into a red paste like Gentleman's Relish. He was an ursine delicacy.

Oh Lord. This was the mind's decay...

Memories of Bering, the brave captain now long dead. Talking bears... A woman dismembered in memory so it was impossible to Frankenstein her. He'd loved that new book by who was it now, Shelley? Something Shelley. He used to remember everything. Now his own name was out of easy grasp.

And in those fading moments his life systems closed, the pulse weakened, the kidneys sundered. The blood flow through his body was staunched as if death was a constellation of tiny dams thrown randomly across the network of tiny rivers.

He lay down, the coma inviting him into its cold parlour. It was comfortable there, the shivering over now because he hadn't the energy to struggle.

Then something happened to Steller.

He saw things.

George Steller, the miraculous naturalist invented television. No, more than that, he invented the television natural history documentary. It flashed in front of his eyes, the whole panoply of creatures he had seen, had himself discovered, not knowing that these would all be named after him. They would be his living breathing testaments out there in the wide world. Even after his death the bird skins he had collected would pass into the hands of other naturalists, people like Pallas the great taxonomist, who would confirm what Steller had found, and name some species after him.

On the small screen of the mind a tight flock of eider, soon to be called Steller's eider flew in tight formation, so very powerful in level flight, achieving speeds of what, fifty miles an hour, maybe more, their wing beats like metronomes. Three male birds flashed by, with their white heads and black monocle markings around the eye, the cinnamon breasts and flanks in contrast with the general grey of the scene.

And then a sea eagle spiralled in, its beak deep and narrow, which often made Steller think its design had something to do with the field of vision, of making sure the beak didn't get in the way of things, get in the line of sight. It was a magnificent specimen, its wings beating what was nothing less than a stentorian clatter in this glacial place, the silence of this film. The huge bird lifted and veered, as if moving away from the cold which was turning the great naturalist into his own statue. A man in a cave. A dying in the dark.

But then the final flourish, a trumpeting, chattering flock of Steller's jays, turning somersaults as they invaded a grove of juniper, stripping berries as if there was no tomorrow.

My, these were fiercely beautiful birds. Steller would have thought something like that but now his brain was so frozen that he could only watch the reels of the documentary unfold this once, in this terrible, endgame viewing, for an audience of one, as if projected onto the wall of the cave.

But they were still there, just, this busy antic band, this species so populous in the thick forests to have a multiplicity of other names. Pine jays. Long crested jays. Mountain jays. But these, the birds in this film, swinging among the cones were Steller's jays. For he is Steller and these sleek, violet-plumaged crows with their punk mohicans were the very life of him.

As if responding to an alarm of some kind, the spotting of a mighty eagle in the vicinity maybe, they shook themselves out of the tree canopy. Then they broke out into open air, like fire smuts lifting up from a firepit. Whirling, burned pieces of paper, they flew upwards and ever up, still chattering as they gained some altitude. And then they stopped, the sky wiped clean of them.

The show was over.

There was one single name on the credits.

That was a given.

The
Murenger

There were customers who came in mainly for the conversation, which was always sharp, urbane and uplifting, others to savour the Imperial Stout with its afternote of Ivory Coast cocoa but there were those who only came in to use the portal, in the way that customers in other, more ordinary pubs used the lavs.

Only last week someone with a burden of heartbreak had borrowed the heavy iron key, pushed open the door, stepped inside and disappeared for a decade. He came back with his hair bleached a startling white snow and when Rob told him he'd only been gone for ten minutes in conventional time the traveller had ordered a triple whisky, downed it in one. 'We're talking sidereal time here,' suggested the time traveller who'd found the whole journey to be hungry work, so ordered four pork pies which he despatched like a wolf eating lapwing chicks.

Rob the publican adored the weird dimensions of the pub, not least after he switched off the till at the end of another evening's civilised roistering. He would then go through into the physic garden, which was really Julie's domain, her healing kingdom.

Julie had planted it according to all the old precepts, with plants arranged according to the ailments they could treat. There was ample hyssop, so good for treating black eyes, not that they got many fisticuffs in the pub, calendula for conjunctivitis and eyebright, as its name suggests, so good for eye conditions that they used to make ale out of it. Maybe they should resurrect the tradition. There was mullein for poultices, growing in high stands, which reminded her that she would need to tie them up soon else they flop over. On one side of the sea-shell path grew clumps of bladder campion and pale drifts of cotton lavender which she usually trimmed with antique shears Rob gave her as a surprise gift. Then there was borage, smelling like an old, tired sea and lovage which had the quiet scent of celery.

At the far end of the garden there was the beginning of a long tunnel linking to a door set into one of the muddiest banks of the River Usk. You would never guess it was there and once it was closed the mud agglutinated around the door, keeping it a secret. This dated back to at least the fifteenth century, when the old apothecaries chose the garden site for its proximity to the river thus making the most of its warm air currents. It gave them a base to moor their herbalists' barge, allowing them to conduct plant-finding expeditions in surrounding areas, most importantly by going upriver and on to the Myddfai hills. Here the famous 'physicians' had started their university of plants, making connections with seats of learning as far away as Sicily and Prague. Rob and Julie had been up there in the bald Welsh hills just three years ago and met an ancient man who looked as if he'd grown up in the Himalayas. He had given Julie three recipes, one of which she was collecting for now.

It was a sloe-black tincture for dealing with the 'Frighteners,' which was another name for delirium tremens. Their customers never got so bad that their dependence on ales and spirits could lead to psychosis and worse but there was a sad old gent who came in one day and he was making his cocktails with methylated spirits and 'Zombie Juice' discount cider and had a fear in his eyes that gave the staff at the Murenger pause. They would have taken him to the Royal Gwent but Julie whispered into Rob's ear that she had the makings of restorative medicine which could banish the horror movies in the old man's skull. Which explained her basket, and the cut harvest of herbs it contained, as she made her way back to the kitchen to concoct the miracle cure. It will be black as bile, as black as a cow's stomach as the Welsh saying has it, *du fel bola buwch*, but it will be as efficacious as can be.

Rob had accessed the special place, an extraordinary part of the Murenger's beyond-conventional-space-and-time dimensionality. Things were there one minute: gone the next. Rob had known one room seemingly to dematerialize, taking the pub cat with it, that was until he remembered they didn't have a cat. So what was it? He looked it up in an old vellum book and discovered the story of the Murenger's wild civet, brought in by a sailor who had sailed six seas and had traded the twisting cat in a hessian sack for intercourse with a monk. They didn't get many monks in nowadays, although they did get a follower of Krishna who was on his way to Neath, selling incense along the way. He sold a bundle of white sage to one customer and a rare bundle of alpine juniper sticks to another, so left even happier than he'd arrived, bidding the assembled company a cheery 'Om' for which he struck a sub-sonic note, like a temple bell, using just his throat and a gulp of air. 'Om,' they replied in a trio of answers.

On quiet nights such as this, drifts of moths would skirtle in, weaving ghost tapestries with the soft needles of their flutter. Lighting the lamps would bring in more, stately drifts of them, some zizzing to death on the open flames. Rob would amble around the garden, pick wormwood, stalks of greater celandine, maybe some comfrey too, if he was minded to make some of his special tea. He could lose himself for hours in there, dreaming of his Malpas republic and pondering how to make it happen. What might be the rallying cry?

Would the people march for him? With him? Without fear in their hearts?

Often, he would then descend to the catacombs, where the spectral butler would nod, a little sanctimoniously as he pushed by, intent on the task in hand. He sometimes helped by changing the barrels, or trapping rodents which gathered where the tunnels met the river. But most often he just went about his business, making and serving tea for the weird crew who lived in the lower rooms. Sometimes, after a hard day of pushing the trolley North North East, South South West and then sometimes down into the Bowels he'd sit down for a moment and if it was quiet – no mice scurrying in the wainscots – no wind keening in the eaves high overhead – he'd close his eyes. Be calm. Control his breaths.

The ghostly butler would be aware that his being, his being-ness was all soft shape and maybe, he would hear that hiss, the quietest hiss as if someone was whispering down a long, long corridor. He might hear the landlord singing in the distance, down the corridor they called 'The Old Silk Road,' gustily bleating out old Malpas Rebel songs about 'Climbing up the 'Barlwm, flags held high.' But if there were no distractions the butler would just sit down a bit heavily and think. Things such as 'I am afloat but not too aware. Yes afloat.' Un-butlery thoughts, more in keeping with the dandelion seed drift of an anchorite in a sea-girt shell. You know the thoughts I mean.

As if the brain was in an aquarium but then the metal frame dissolves and water fills all the space. Around him the faint hiss of water, filling his nose and throat.

That then was his deepest sense of what he was.

A butler yes, but also a floating awareness, in an aquarium without a frame. Or glass.

He was a brain precariously perched, his skull a cave to harbour thoughts that clanged emptily, like the old bells of a mountain monastery.

He was the hollowness in things.

Sometimes he doubted his existence. Rob might one day see the butler and greet him as if he were composed of flesh and blood and another walk on by as if he were transparent, or more spectral than he cared to be. He would go up to him as he was changing a cask of bitter and ask him straight. 'Do you know I am here? And if you do, how do you prove it? You could bite me, maybe, take an anch out of my arm. Or just touch me, feel me, use your touch to confirm that I am here and in this space. Or maybe this beer cellar is Plato's cave and we are just shadow puppets.'

The butler knew that Rob read a lot and so could help him expand his lexicon. He would ask for words and Rob would give him some, choice ones in keeping with the wandering world of the ghostly butler.

Miscreant. Archbishop. Nincompoop.

But the words were there and had range and compass and he could map out his world, this Murenger House as the upstairs dwellers called it, the topers and imbibers who would never hear the tiny silver bells down below, ringing to bring Darjeeling to someone in the Bowels, or up the in dovecote where all those pigeons make such a smell, or the room that no-one dares go in. Rooms beyond rooms beyond rooms.

The butler's hands were heavy from pushing. So much hot water, rickety piles of expensive crockery, the eighteen teas blended, from powerful Ceylon to tiny green leaves picked high in the Hindu Kush.

Upstairs they have central heating. Down here the place gets cold in winter, it's a draughty pile. Whoever said ghosts don't feel the cold. The grave is a fridge, the nether-realms like the freezer section of Iceland. All the draughts. He can feel them on the sensitive parts... the nape of the neck, the palm.

And he makes them, starts them off, sends them up the stairwells to force old men in mufflers in the back room to comment on the chill. He may fan an old newspaper, start a draught in that way.

Or he starts the draughts with his heavy breath and if he wanted to he could start a gale.

Whoo-oo. Whoo-ooo.

And set off draughts so strong that they would push on through this ancient pile. Unsettle the foundations. Scare the mice so that they shake.

And blow away all the shadows.

Rob likes the butler as much as he enjoys the green smell of the physic garden, when he's picking leaves for the teapot. They are his secrets, not mentioned in the lease. This public house is about so much more than beer.

One. Two. Three. Rob makes sure the coast is clear and steps out into the bar area, hiding the key in the alcove.

One of the regulars asks for pickled eggs and he thinks that there were days when they probably served up curlew eggs, harvested from rush pockets out on the Levels. Times change, he knew, and in the Murenger they could also overlap. Sidereal time, too, that most certainly applied to this amazing hostelry. Measuring time in terms of the earth's rotation against certain fixed stars. Better than a digital watch according to some of his more learned customers.

He poured another pint of ambrosial liquid, which brought a tear to the eye of one customer. Steff was back from his Italian travels, ordering sausage and mash.

Rob looked around, at the people making the quiet music of companionship and conversation, supping ales.

He looked at the jar behind him. Pickled eggs, eh? How specific are man's desires. He rang the bell to announce day's end.

Fire with Fire

As anyone who plays with matches knows a fire simply wants to grow. Even the smallest has ambitions – to graduate as an out of control conflagration, devouring all. But each one starts small, with a spark, a light, a breath of flame. Ask any arsonist.

This one started classically enough, as an accident, a cigarette tossed heedlessly out of a car window which then settled in a tuffet of dry grass. Some desiccated stalks soon caught and then, in turn torched neighbouring stalks. Soon there was a purple fuse running along the hedge base, snuffling around, seeking oxygen, dry understory, blaze fuel.

And this is how The Great Fire of Surrey started. By the time it was reported it was already being encouraged by the wind, egged on by an unseasonal south westerly and growing uncommonly fierce, with great tiger tails of flame and licks of fire burning a Halloween orange.

The silver birches of Ranmore were fiercely ablaze and the whipping wind fed their ignitions, sweeping the heat and fury ever on and on. Stunned villagers in Tilford watched helplessly as their famous oak – which had stood there like a custodial spirit for nigh on eight hundred years – turned into a terrible green and red bonfire, even as the nearby cricket hut blew up. Then they had to look to their own possessions, save what they could. Meanwhile the wildfire charged on – a burning juggernaut turning the world into ash.

Teams of firemen worked tirelessly but they were neither equipped for such fires nor did they understand them. Grass fires, yes, gorse fires occasionally, but this was like something you saw on TV. They were out of their depth: it was out of their league.

In the emergency services call centre they were inundated with adrenaline-charged callers, their voices shrill with fear.

'I'd like to report a fire, well a bloody big fire.'

'Could you please confirm your location caller?'

'Bourne Wood, near Farnham. Never seen anything like it.'

'Is anyone in immediate danger? Is it near any housing?'

'It's headed for the nursing home. Can't be more than half a mile away from it.'

'Do you know the name of the home, sir?'

'The Laurels.'

'I'm dispatching someone now, sir. Thank you, sir. Please keep yourself safe, evacuate the area.'

The next caller was curt, short and to the point.

'It's the apocalypse. It's come to Oxshott.'

In truth it was hard to dispatch someone to Oxshott, as they could only cover half the calls they'd lodged. The shift organiser was pulling his hair out. The calls came as flurries and the team leaders were screeching like parakeets. He considered taking the staff off the phones and into the small canteen where they could all pray. Maybe *it really was* the apocalypse, coming without trumpets.

It seemed as if the entire county'd caught fire, hit by blankets of napalm, frazzling tree and copse and thicket. Hawthorn hedges burned like fuses, the flames running along field-sides before turning corners and changing direction. It was a sight to strike fear into hearts.

A wildfire! In Surrey! Little wonder that there were news helicopters overhead, with endless live reports from above the smoke palls and ash clouds.

The Emergency Cobra cabinet meeting was chaired by a Prime Minister who looked drained before it started. There was enough political catastrophe to be getting on with, electoral landslides and the fervid spread of populism without natural disasters.

'Anyone know what we do about this?' she asked in a plaintive voice, an appeal like a heart surgeon who'd found something the size of a peanut in a aorta and had forgotten everything she'd been taught in medical school.

'I'd ask the Americans. They have plenty of experience. Too much experience if anything.'

'Don't ask the President though,' suggested the Chancellor. 'He doesn't believe in global warming. He'd say these were fires were fake, fake news.'

The map on the whiteboard showed several emergencies. In west Wales a peat bog was burning like a Biblical curse. There'd been a surge in substantial grass fires all over the place not to mention several big swathes of grouse moor ablaze in the Peak District and in Yorkshire. But the fire in Surrey was by far the worst as there were so many villages and towns at risk.

'I never thought there were so many trees in the south of England,' said the Prime Minister.

'Which explains the request to release all but three fire trucks from Gatwick Airport. You'll need to sign this...' said a grimacing civil servant, lackeying toward her with a form.

The woman who stood in front of them, asserted her authority unfussily. Amber Hill had flown in on a red-eye from New Jersey, leaving a dinner party for her eldest daughter's eighteenth birthday to catch the flight after taking the call, which came directly from the White House. Hill was the most famous firefighter in America, stepping metaphorically into Red Adair's boots, with their nitrile rubber soles. He'd fought oil rig fires: she fought forest. Her use of language was at first a trifle perplexing, with terms such as 'burning out' and 'backburns,' bright examples of two nations being divided by a common language.

The Englanders were getting used to Americans jetting in to take control, what with the new London Crime Commissioner who'd arrived from working the South Chicago beat and had started on day one encouraging the use of knuckle-dusters.

'Many of you will think we fight the big fires with aerial drops, helicopters with payloads of water or fire resistant foam. But that's just the TV pictures. We fight the fires as best we can on the ground and whereas you fight fire with water we use the fire itself. We fight fire with fire. That's what we'll be doing.'

She pointed out possible control lines and suggested ways to deploy the men. They'd be hard pressed to find the numbers, but with Downing Street involved they'd be able to draft in people from other counties, other countries even.

'You'll find it counterintuitive at first to set a controlled blaze but if it's downwind of the main fire, you can push the blaze toward the main fire and it'll eat up all the fuel in between. This is where I'm suggesting we set the main lines.' She showed them a map of Waverley borough, deftly shining a laser pen to show how to use natural features to help, not to mention the river courses. 'Each fire,' she continued, 'has its own character, like the lead actor in a film, or the main player in a novel. It can be belligerent, stubborn, cunningly intelligent, or a sociopath.'

'What's this one then?' asked one of the men in the room.

'Too soon to tell. Give me a few hours. Now where are the new satellite pictures and the Met Office stuff?'

In a glade overshadowed by evergreen box trees the fire was, at that point, a crumpled figure hunched over, seemingly intent on lighting a cigarette, cupping the glowing end away from the breeze. With an emphysemic struggle of breath it blew on the tip, making it glow, the paper rim sputtering. It then applied its glow to a small pile of leaf brush, getting it going with a Boy Scout enthusiasm, enjoying its tiny flare before feeding it with twigs and then fanning it with an outsize leaf of Chinese rhubarb. The fire caught, started snaking along a ghyll, one of those sharp ravines that bisected this touristy landscape. Nature was an arsonist, using lightning or serendipitous spark like striking a Zippo.

After number punching and doing the diagnostics Amber decided it was time to get out into the field and so she joined an already haggard looking set of firemen who were trying to beat back the fire with forestry brushes. She showed them how to burn out a section and once they'd got the hang of it they started to read the fire for themselves, to imagine its hunger and work out ways of denying it food.

The fire was by now a braggart, a swaggering swashbuckler, all attitude and strut, like that Adam and the Ants video from back in the day. It shook firebrand diamonds loose from its dreadlocks, which hit the ground as small plosions, setting light to brush and tindersticks in a circle. The dervish figure enjoyed its deadly dance, its fire-starting mazurka. It twirled, dementedly, mocking the insect-men who stood in its way.

The infant offspring of the main fire had now dispersed like mushroom spores, tiny embers that managed to contain a firefly glow even as they parachuted hither and thither. Some of the lucky ones settled on dry tussocks, or patches of mossy kindling and glowed desperately, with just a few seconds left, if that, needing a breeze to kindle and encourage flame. It only took one spark, say, to nestle with a hiss of blue flame in a pile of lawn trimmings to set a new blaze running and it was astonishing how soon one grew, consuming anything in its path – any tinder, discarded bus ticket, a pile of flammable litter.

It was an exhausting day.

In the car which sped her to her hotel Amber pondered this latest job, tackling the English beast, a worrisome creature so completely out of control and all the more so for being in a land where wildfires were unknown. Which was why the local firemen, the brigades of Surrey Fire and Rescue couldn't handle it for all their bravery and daring do.

A fire was sentient. Even as she unpacked her case she felt its awareness of her. She was a hare in open country, noted by the fire, that fox, that wily wolf, who calculated its best and stealthiest approach. She was its nemesis and so it wanted to burn her alive.

Amber didn't know how much more she could take, or give as she'd been parachuted into three major disaster zones in so many months and had seen such grave and terrible destructions – lives lost by the hundred, homes turned into charcoaled wasteland, household pets charred in their kennels and cages. She had been in northern California where the town of Paradise turned into hell and she could still picture in the mind's eye the old woman fried to a crisp and the remains of a metal rocking chair on the porch where she would have sat, immobile perhaps as her end came as a sheet of flame and diabolic smoke. Homes became pyres, burning ghats of clapperboard.

She had just returned to her room when she got a call, asking for guidance on two new outbreaks and she was amazed to see the locations, each an easy mile from any previous fire.

They had turned a Travelodge into a temporary headquarters and when she returned there that night she could see lines of men, hunched with exhaustion coming in over some stubble fields. It was an oil painting, their outlines pinkened by the westering sun. They looked like she felt but she had to find the energy to ring home. It had been a full-on day and the fire had been wayward and impetuous, setting off in zig-zags, running lines that confused her until she charted the geography of the hills and the direction of the wind, seeing gulleys where it would accelerate, scoops of land where it would power on.

Despite the cloying weariness she Facetimed her daughter who told her all about the project in school in which they all made drums and shared the fact she'd managed to make the chequer pattern in the Rubik's cube all by herself and how she was going for a sleepover with Amy Mac and Amy Mac had promised they would stay up all night and have popcorn as they watched Princess Diaries for the hundredth time. When the call was over she felt happy that Maisie was staying with the Mackays as they were level headed people and would find a way of encouraging even two young girls who were pumped up with sugar to get enough sleep and not be vegetative by the time they went to school.

She went into the bar on impulse, needing something to cool down her overheated brain. No-one said a word about her attire, or the soot covering her face and she ordered a beer, a large one. She could have done without the man on the bar stool next along who wanted to start up a conversation but then again everyone was excited by all the action and wanted to know everything. And this one was obviously a news hawk who watched all the bulletins as he already knew her name before she grudgingly introduced herself...

'What you do is so, well elemental.'

If he hadn't used that word she would have found some excuse to leave the counter but it was not only uncommon in the context but also exactly the word she used herself about what she did.

Because that's how she often saw it, what she did in life. It might be a tussle, a wrestle or sometimes a battle against a fire. It might rage and bluster but she would dominate it, outflank it, assert her control. At times it would be a chess game, her bid to intellectually outwit the fire as if it was a sentient thing, plotting to go this way or that, her finding a way to block it, turn it, box it into an oxygen-depleted corner.

Elemental. Her against an element, the last woman standing against the burning wall of flame. It was only a word, but so uncommonly used that she found herself accepting the offer of another drink, and even though she knew she had to get up in a brief few hours she found herself talking to this man, whose name was Pete and who had piercing blue eyes.

The early morning reports were not encouraging, not least because they made her aware of how poorly equipped the place was to deal with such a fire. She'd asked about helicopter water drops, or aircraft carrying huge, liquid payloads, but they didn't have a single one. In the whole of the UK, and even though one of her colleagues said they could probably borrow something from Spain it was the way he'd said it that had caused her most alarm, the sense that he didn't see the point in bringing in the heavy armour as this was England, and they knew how to sort things out, stiff upper lip, Dunkirk spirit and all that. Turned out the man was an urban planner, had only got into this line of work because he couldn't find any other. She made the formal request and he slumped off to get on with it.

Overnight the fire had razed four hundred acres beyond what had been yesterday's confinement zone, so it had jumped some of the clear-paths that had been bulldozed through to protect the most vulnerable properties. The evacuations had been conducted smoothly though, and the police had only had to arrest a dozen or so householders who refused to leave their homes stuffed with family mementos and antique treasures.

Amber asked Brogan, the head of the Surrey Fire Brigade for an update on the new fires they were setting and he shamefacedly admitted that his men hadn't really known what they were doing, or had failed to understand the instructions so had waited until she'd arrived. Without a moment's hesitation she put on her outsize jacket, picked up a helmet and said they would visit the main blaze together.

The fire was by now a juggernaut. It had accelerated as she slept for those brief few hours, the southern England gusts acting like the Santa Ana winds in Southern California, whipping it up, driving it on. The whole of Box Hill was ablaze and the switch in wind direction threatened to extend its reach out onto the big heaths to the west. Luckily the main road cutting south from Leatherhead made an effective fire break, especially now that traffic had been stopped from using it because of the thick drifts of smoke. It was still busy with emergency vehicles. As he drove Brogan apologized that the helicopter he'd requisitioned was in the machine shop undergoing repairs but that some Army choppers were on their way and would be available to them by late morning.

'What I can't understand,' he said, 'is how this fire is spreading so easily. There are fields and things in between the big stands of trees, surely those should be enough to slow it down.'

Amber had the answer on her tablet, open on the key maps of woodland holdings in the county. While the man beside her might have seen open spaces and therefore hurdles to the flow, she saw green connections, places where the flames could jump from the crowns of tall trees to others, contoured lines which showed where the firesurge could hurry. She knew the fire was willful, impetuous, sneaky but that didn't mean you couldn't read it, second-guess it by artfully reading the lie of the land.

'We have to contain Waverley,' Amber suggested, marrying up the truth of the map and the data that had come in overnight. 'Fires, eh? It's so much easier dealing with them in buildings. At least then you know where the flames are. Up country they can creep up behind you, catch you unawares.'

She traced her fingers across the lines of the OS map, dragging more info into view. This was one of the biggest swathes of trees in the whole of the county, an incendiary mix of old box and yew and ash not to mention the old coppices which had run wild. She knew her tree species and she knew which ones were the ones to watch. At home it was the eucalypts, explosive with oils, that could blow with all the force of dynamite once they'd cooked up to plosive heat. Here the box trees burned with oxyacetylene intensity. The ash with enormous vigour. She remembered the words of Peregrine, her old professor in college in Idaho whose mantra was 'Flammability is determined by ignition, sustainability, combustibility and consumability.' She could see in the mind's eye the fire moving through the leaf litter, now tinderbox dry, pretty much undetected until it flamed at some unexpected point.

'We're getting reports that some of the big garden hedges are going up like daddy-o especially the Leylandii. And that grows everywhere, one of those green screens that allows an Englishman's home to be his castle.'

Amber registered his words but was puzzling over the day's approach. On the sunrise satellite pictures there seemed to be three main fires at Mole Valley, Elmbridge and the biggest one at Waverley. Here they'd had to evacuate four whole villages in as many hours. The operation had been commendably swift for an evac, moving a lot of old people from Tilford and Dunsfold, Alfold and Peper Harow but the firefighting effort simply wasn't sufficient to stem the blazing tide and there had been millions of pounds' worth of damage as many of these houses were worth millions in themselves. They'd failed to stop the fire reaching two of those, even though the fact hadn't been reported yet, due to the news curfew 'for operational reasons.' In truth it was to keep the news choppers and intrepidly keen journalists from getting in the way as the fire grew brash, arrogant, megalomane.

When she got back to the Lodge that night the firemen had doused the place with water as it stood in the path of a fire they struggled to contain. The whole place glistened as if covered in snail trail. She looked quickly in the bar but Pete wasn't there, but the barman spotted her and beckoned her over to give her a small parcel. Inside it was a novel by William Maxwell, the one Pete had mentioned the night before, proclaiming it his favourite. There was also a note, saying 'See you tomorrow' in handwriting which was open and bold. Before she went to sleep she read one whole sentence before being embraced by the arms of Morpheus. 'In order to pay off an old debt that someone else had contracted, Austin King had said yes when he knew that he ought to have said no, and now at five o clock on a July afternoon he saw the grinning face of trouble everywhere he turned.'

In her dreams that night tendrils of flame snaked in toward her legs wanting to catch hold of her, to charcoal her skin, to crisp her eyes.

All over the Surrey Hills trees turned fierce lanterns as boughs and branches flared – from piney twigs through knotted growths to arthritic limbs, all catching light and flaring like phosphorus flares. Even the prickly mass of evergreen foliage in the hollows caught fire quickly despite the seeping damp of early summer, with its torrents of rain. Three weeks of punishing sun had been enough to dry out the countryside. The arboreal blaze incandesced as every green leaf, moss beard and crabapple was consumed. The rising sap converted into rocket fuel and berries, such as the black pips of the elder, boiled swiftly before bursting with a fizz. Acorns and beech mast simply exploded, scattering tiny shrapnel of hard shells across a wide area.

Day three and the fire was a land grab. Abinger Roughs and Friday Street were engulfed. The hamlet of Pease Pottage was under imminent threat. It was some kind of Armageddon.

Amber was kept going by adrenaline and caffeine but the relentless march of the fire, its switchbacks and U turns, its crazy whims were defeating her. She had too much data, too few men on the ground and the helicopters from Spain were a day away, a dozen Airbus choppers equipped with Bambi buckets that could scoop up a huge litre-age of water at a time and these could make use of village ponds at places such as Buckland, Chiddingfold and Coleshill, taking away a payload complete with tadpoles and fish. The RAF Sea Kings which had just arrived did their bit but Amber and her team needed these more maneouvurable craft to deal with the number of fires in play. Over a hundred at present: new ones sighted every hour.

She got out into the field again in the morning, barking orders, taking control. The breathing equipment was old fashioned, hints of the Second World War about some of the stuff. Masks like tin cans. Cumbersome oxygen tanks so big she suspected they'd come off trolleys.

She got a ride to the biggest control line, the one they had to hold else the fire marched on a big town and fried its edges. There were petrol stations in its way, underground reservoirs set to blow. Brogan was in a huddle of exhausted men, poring over a paper map, swigging water. She left him to it and went to scout out things for herself. She could feel the temperature rise, prickling a sweat on her skin. In front of her was the epicentre of the fire, burning an intense tangerine and sending out heat like a miniature sun.

If life were a movie this was be the climactic ending, the fire a computer-generated humanoid with more than a hint of Hellraiser about him, scaly arms with muscles like hills and wearing a great cloak of fire, draped with sulphur yellow ribbons and comet tails of incandescence and blaze. And she was all that stood between it and the high school or the hospital or nursing home, whatever vulnerable community the screenwriter had placed right behind her. And it swelled up in size and consequence and menace, bulking up, mushrooming in wraps of fug and smoke.

In the real world Amber was aware that she was entirely alone as the clearance squads had disappeared over to her left, taking down brash and clearing dark thickets of primary growth. She'd have beaten an orderly retreat from the wall of flame which was encroaching at a lick across the yardage of dry heath but then she saw the man on the floor, a fireman who'd fallen down and seemed to be out for the count. He was the other side of the flamewall, but his yellow helmet stood out against the smudged charcoal of the newly burned heath. To get to him she would have to go round the fire or go straight through and she wasn't wearing the right clothes for that and neither was there a source of water to douse what she was wearing to give her any chance to scythe her way through the flames. Even in the seconds since she'd spotted him the fire had advanced twenty yards.

Elemental. That sort of tussle.

She had to face down a pure element to get to this man on the ground and even as she took a few paces back before running through the curtain of fire she glimpsed her daughter's eyes, heard her father's voice. She conflated all the fires she'd challenged as one impossible blaze. This one. She took a huge draught of oxygen deep into her lungs and prayed she could pick up enough speed to leap through to the other side.

But in mid air came the realization that the flames were too wide and she fell into a mass of burning elder, the flames searing off the branches like magnesium flares. A tripwire of briar roots had brought her down into Hades. It was her last stumble in this life, as her fireman's death came swiftly and her body was taken by that dangerous trinity: the overwhelming gases, the disrobing flames, the silencing heat.

Just as there is a kiss of life so too there is a kiss of death. The fire approached her on a rake, as if kneeling down. It sucked the air out of her lungs, deflating the very alveolae of her.

In the city of Reading Pennsylvania there would be a statue to her. Once a year, year on year you might chance upon a young girl turning into a woman as she made her annual pilgrimage. People used to get onto tiptoe in order to kiss the bronze cheek as a sign of luck and it was burnished there and the young woman used to kiss the fingers too, as if she could summon her mother back to life.

On one visit, by rare coincidence, there was a fire in a warehouse across the river and its lights were reflected in the curves of the statue, giving it sheen and flicker. It made the girl think deeply, about her firefighter mother, who was boundlessly brave and would face down any fire. It gave her an idea, a path for herself, even as the lunging flames broke out of a series of windows. They were powerful enough to light up her mother's metal face, even at this distance, transmuting the greening metal, giving it the pulsing lustre of human skin. Her daughter looked at the jut of the bronze jaw and saw, in full understanding that she was the same, that a certain heroic stubbornness had been handed on in the genes. Something burning brightly within.

Candles

Daniels had grown a tad too interested in his own research and now he couldn't sleep at night, his eyes grown owl-like, globular and staring. He would sleep a fitful couple of hours in the chair in the afternoon, but nights were for fretting about what he had learned, and, more troublingly, what he was proposing to do with the knowledge.

A folklorist wouldn't have normally expected to travel through such ghoulish terrain because of his work, but there he was now, doomed to walk in the ghastliest of places. And it wasn't normal.

It started as a book exercise, reading his way through all the available literature in the Salisbury collection about corpse candles, those strange apparitions of the dead that manifested themselves in lonely cottages, busy farmsteads, indeed wherever a person was about to die. Just a candle, in a window, moving without human agency. It presaged the passing – gave a glimpse, perhaps – of when the soul would leave the mortal cage of rib and heart, when the candle of life was snuffed out, dispatched by a quick finger pinch.

Carmarthenshire, the old Carmarthenshire, was one of the epicentres of activity and there were still many old people who had seen a candle, and only they were qualified to say what age the dead person would be, a matter of some consequence in a farm, say, with many living souls, including the servants, who were often tubercular.

A small candle for a child, a brief light.
A larger candle for an adult, its flame guttering as if in a draught.
A white candle for a woman.
A red one for a man.

It was all somehow classified just as surely as it was preordained.

Daniels visited seven old people's homes, with his voice recorder and his notebook, detailing apparitions from Pendine to Llansawel, thin illuminations in the conifered valleys of Brechfa and candles manifest in cottages high in the high sheep folds above Rhandirmwyn. He also visited farmers in isolated tenancies, and dutifully recorded both their sightings and responses to them, and as he did so he realized just how lucky he was to have done the work now, when all these people were still alive. Five years more, ten years certainly, and they would all have been dead, their recollections turned to gossamer.

Daniels' desire to see a corpse candle for himself grew more and more. He volunteered to work in a hospice just outside Llandeilo, and put his name down, time and time again for the night shift, but to no avail. Then one of the other volunteers moved to Birkenhead and he was asked to cover.

Then came the awful realisation. It came as a flash, an unbidden epiphany (as if there's any other kind), that these people didn't just die but, rather had been killed, and those who saw the candles were manifesting their own dark and troubled consciences.

And so he knew how he could see one: his own corpse candle.

One morning he was reading the Reverend D.G.Williams' collection of

Carmarthenshire folk literature, about how unwise it was to interfere with the passage of a corpse candle if it passed in front of you: a blacksmith, *William John y gof,* was struck down mortally from his horse when he tried to stop a candle crossing open ground in front of him – and of the three candles seen in the waters of the river near Golden Grove. Later that same night three coach travellers were claimed by the black waters. Daniels realised that he would have to murder to satisfy his folklorist's deepening interest in the subject.

So that Thursday, on the night shift, he stole all the makings of a lethal injection from the pharmacy cupboard. He identified Meryl Williams, aged ninety-one and demented as can be, as someone with no real quality of life, his only flimsy justification for what he was about to do. And having hidden the syringe, and secreted the phial of Fentanyl – sometimes served in lollipops to cancer sufferers – he sat in the comfortable chairs in the conservatory to wait for the flicker.

When it came he had no idea he was watching the last illuminating moments of his own life's journey, the candle burning defiantly, as if casually aware of that one last glorious gasp of sudden and transpiring air. He sat there staring at the candle, reached out to hold it. Found that he could, and that it seemed to guide him. Into that terrible terrain, that moss filled bog, haunted by the shades of all the other would be murderers. His fellow travellers. Each clutching his own brief light, as if seized in an iron vice of complete and utter fear.

Oology

'Suddenly something came out of the land, some cool shiver of Spring...'

The Serpent, Neil Gunn

It might have been that May breath, that long exhalation of balmier wind coming up the river valleys, the Tay, the Ness, the Findhorn, the one that makes the alder leaves shake. Midges like drifts of pollen, fidgeting in huge droves, swarming in Brownian motion. Darts of trout in pebbly shallows. A kingfisher unloosing an azure arrow. This a time of brightening light that encourages bud and blossom and dials birdsong up to the fullest trill.

Naomi felt the new warmth through her many layers of clothing, even as she vowed that this would be her last year of fieldwork. Bloody midges. She was getting too old for this: she needed to settle down, have children, be able to access a hot shower 24/7. She certainly did not want to spend her time in caravans drinking tea with nature nuts. That was her name for recently graduated conservationists willing to endure drilling cold, beating rain and battering weather, all in the ____ ___ that through their efforts they could save the ___ ____ually in their twenties and she was now a good ___ ___ould have children. They still were.

___ sent down streamers of light through the tree

75

canopy and the temperature increased again, albeit slightly – just a small calibration but sufficient to change her mood. She had plenty to do, anyway.

She had to check the nets for starters. There were four mist nets set up in two long glades, set there to catch small birds for ringing. If she was lucky there'd be crested tits, the sole reason she got paid for the work but usually it would be anything but. There might be blue tits, blackbirds and, on one red-letter day a male sparrowhawk wrapped up in the nets. It fixed her with a gimlet eye and drew blood when she took it out of the pouch of netting. Its eyes were remarkable, a bright traffic light yellow.

Naomi had now spent three seasons researching the trees best favoured by the cresteds, found they doted on Scotch pine and avoided spruce. The point of the exercise was to explore ways of joining up the populations in the Spey and Dee water catchments. These were separated by empty areas of wild country, so tree corridors would help this sparky little species that was sedentary to say the least. The tits seldom flew far from home, which meant their range tended to stay the same size. They needed encouragement to move further and a few lodgepole pines or larches wouldn't go amiss. In the hand they were attractive birds, with bridled faces and tight little zebra markings on the crest. And rare, too. A twitcher from London had got so excited by seeing two crested tits in a glade in Aviemore that he had had an aneurysm on the spot.

On the way back from the nets Naomi noted a stand of fine silvery rowans. She was keen to recommend in her report the planting of this species, and imagined it could be a commercial crop here in the Highlands if harvested intelligently. Half the berries left on the trees for the birds, half for human use – stewing rowan jam and jellies and she plumped for the brand name 'Red Rowan' which had a simple lilt to it, like Rob Roy. She had even designed a mock label for the it with a drawing of a redwing astride a bouquet of berries.

One of the old gamekeepers, his face turned mahogany by the weather, had told her that the old folk always planted a rowan in front of a home to keep the evil spirits away. She'd planted a berry in a pot and it was already a green twig of a thing, able to ward off very small demons. The wizened man had given her a blue ribbon as a gift, made of discards of wool, explaining that the little folk of the Highlands who danced wildly around Hallow Fires, made knots in strands of wool like these which they then threw over their shoulders. If someone became fascinated by them they would be entirely in their thrall.

She was told by text that a Finnish researcher would be joining her for a month and that he'd be using the other caravan if that was OK. She bristled at the fact she'd have to move all her bits and pieces into one van. At the same time she welcomed the company, even if it was someone whose name she couldn't pronounce. She looked again at the text message and tried to twist her tongue around it. Väinämöinen Lehikoinen. Male? Female? Human would be a start.

Her recent record was not seeing a single soul for nine seemingly eternal days. It suited some people – this ascetic, hermit's life – but not her. She needed news, conversation, hell's teeth an argument with someone if it could run to that.

He arrived on the Tuesday when she was shopping down in Inverness and by the time she was back he was sitting on the step of the van reading a book. He introduced himself with a captivating smile and Naomi felt a frisson inside. He had eyes like deep blue pools and the book in his hand was a volume of poetry. Not to mention the fact that he asked if it was OK to make bread in the morning. This one was a keeper. Shame he was going back in four weeks.

They had a great first day together, as his arrival coincided with the monthly capercaillie count, for which they had divided a big patch of land into transects to be walked by forty volunteers. It took them out into some of her favourite places, great sweeps of land with jagged dentitions of granite breaking up the ridges. She and Vee saw a big male bird cannoning out of a new plantation and the others brought back news of a burgeoning population. They all built a fire and drank Scotch in the open air, called themselves the Capercaillie Squad as the sunset turned into a scarlet mackerel sky.

By the time they got back to the 'vans they were too exhausted to cook, so Vee suggested they should get a cab into town.

'There's no phone signal, I'm afraid. This is like the dark side of the moon.'

'There is a signal in the pub. I checked. We could walk there, have a drink and then get a taxi.'

Naomi hadn't been in a taxi for years. She hadn't been to a pub with a man for years and she was discombobulated by the prospect.

Vee'd chosen McBains Restaurant by the River by using Trip Advisor and Naomi felt her clothes were all wrong for the place. They both laughed at the fact they chose the same starter and main course but the food was superb, especially as Naomi'd been surviving on Pot Noodle and digestive biscuits in the main.

It was a tremendous meal, with Vee quoting beautiful lines from the poetry of Mary Oliver and their life stories were soon flowing in tandem with the wine. The one he'd ordered had been evidence enough of how different he was.

'This is a real find,' he'd proclaimed, showing the label, the Maturano.

'It comes from a little valley called Val Comino in Lazio. This one's made by a family called the Farinellis who own a vineyard in Alvito. Giovanni Farinelli is a fine old fellow and he's very proud of this wine because Maturano is an ancient native variety of grape.'

'You know him then, this Giovanni?'

'No. It's just one of my interests. Indigenous wine varieties of Italy. I could be on a TV quiz, have it as my chosen subject...'

The wine was orange in colour and mustily delicious, like sipping autumn.

They were on the second bottle – the one that ensures deep secrets are unloosed – when Naomi saw him.

'Shit,' she said, 'that's him,' slumping her head away from the man in question, so that he wouldn't realise he'd been spotted.

Sitting on a table in the corner by himself was Connor, the worst egg collector in the land, and self-styled as the 'last of the great oologists.' He was a scourge, a nemesis to those who wanted to protect rare birds. Life for him was all about swelling the size of the collection, the serried ranks of drawers full of eggs, from red backed shrikes, corn buntings, hobbies, merlins.

Naomi's employers had circulated photos of him at the beginning of last season and they had actually caught him with a clutch of dotterel eggs which he'd stolen from a scrape of a nest in the high Cairngorms but it had been too late to return them to safety. However, he'd got away with it in court, owing to a technicality in his arrest that his fat cat lawyer did his best to successfully exploit.

As she spooned syllabub into her mouth she explained all this to Vee and said they had to do something.

'We could be detectives...' said Vee with a schoolboy grin. '... Follow him without his knowing. I think we can do that. I think I packed the mantle of invisibility when I left Helsinki.'

She laughed that she could imagine this captivating man owning such a garment.

'So what should we do?'

'Just keep an eye on him until he leaves, and I'll book a cab to wait down the street. I'll tail him, like they do in the movies.'

'They're going to love that in Inverness... follow that car. They'll just think you're taking the piss.'

'I'll find out where he's staying and we'll take it from there. Heck, I can't say I can remember a dinner date quite so exciting. Great food, great company and now the thrill of the chase...'

'What do you want me to do?'

'Get ready for tomorrow.'

She looked at him a tad blankly.

'He'll be on the move. People like this don't hang around. The more time they spend in a place the more likely they are to be identified if something goes wrong. Get all the maps ready, so we can be right on his tail.'

'In a cab? We'll be as visible as hell.'

'Leave that to me. I have a mate who has a Land Rover. I'll see if I can get the keys. We're a resourceful lot the Finns,' he said, enjoying the tangerine tinges of the last of the wine.

'This is divine, Vee, thanks very much for choosing it,' licking her lips discretely.

Meanwhile Connor was finishing an outsize porterhouse steak.

As they left the restaurant Vee gave Naomi a little blue ribbon. 'Here, wear this, it'll bring you luck.'

When the egg collector slunk off into the night Vee was on his tail, while Naomi got the same cab driver they'd had earlier to take her back to the caravan.

'How was it?' he asked her, perked up by the evening's unexpected fares.

'Best dinner date ever,' said Naomi, still splicing together quotes from the night, not least of which was 'great company.' She hadn't had a meal as good as this one for, well, forever.

Before she lost the phone signal she got in touch with the species protection officer back at HQ and he sounded genuinely thrilled to hear they'd spotted Connor. The man used words such as 'ascertain' in that way that made Naomi certain that he was a former policeman.

In the morning Naomi and Vee were sitting around the corner from

Connor's B&B, in a Land Rover belonging to a local fishery and thus emblazoned with paintings of outsize salmon and trout, trying to be inconspicuous.

Connor appeared in T-shirt and jeans but once he was in the car he exchanged these for camouflage gear.

'You'd have thought he was off to Helmand not the Highlands,' said Vee with an untypical sneer. 'Still, if he means business we mean business. Any sign of your man from HQ?'

'He's two hours away apparently.'

'So, it's up to us then.'

Connor's rental car scorched away while Vee got used to the gearsticks on the Discovery. He was not adept at tailing cars, keeping out of the driver's rear-view mirror. As the land climbed it became near impossible to keep behind him but Naomi played a hunch. They took the left-hand fork where Connor took the right and headed out over a long stretch of open country, where twisted trees had been bonsaied by the whipping wind.

'I know where he's going,' said Naomi, giving Vee instructions about which turns to take. 'He's after the eagles.'

It had been the first time for eagles to nest in this part of Scotland for many years and Naomi was one of the few people who knew the exact location, a wild crag that commanded a view of the whole world. How on earth had Connor known about it? Inside job, had to be. In fact, there could only be six people on the planet who knew about this nesting site.

There were points during the chase when they could see Connor's car in the far distance and luckily Naomi knew this patch of land like the back of her hand.

They were lucky that Connor chose to do his egg collecting solo, as by the time they arrived at the site he had already starting lowering himself down a rope which he'd tied onto the bole of a birch.

Naomi asked Vee what they were going to do, as the man

would reach the nest in just a few minutes' time. The female bird had already left the edge and was shrieking overhead, its enormous wings flapping up a gale as it circled above the fanatical thief.

'Only one thing for it,' answered Vee, taking out a pocketknife and walking up to the rope, making a sawing action.

'You can't,' said Naomi, 'that would be murder.'

'Is it murder if taking a life means saving the lives of so many birds?'

'But they're birds,' argued Naomi, 'just birds.'

Vee cut strands of the tense rope and they pinged free.

'Now tell him we're cutting the rope. He'd have felt that give.'

Naomi was just about to shout down when the eagle swooped, its talons agape and even though she didn't have a clean line of sight she heard a man's voice, screaming as he fell.

Connor, who had always studied birds, had now become one, a peregrine in a stoop, falling like a lead ball.

Naomi looked at Vee, before they both peered over the edge to where lay the splayed and broken body.

They then looked back at the dangling end of rope, broken at the place of the first cut, the fibres frayed in all directions.

This would take some explaining...

The dead man.

The cut rope.

The settling eagle, its huge wings shadowing its golden brood of dangerous eggs.

Age,
That Old Haven

Carol had never felt so alive, playing squash at hyper-speed, her heart almost fibrillating with exertion. The rubber ball resounded so fast it thrummed with the sound of very distant thunder, the very air molecules zinging in the quick air. It was a game so fast it was hard to keep score but luckily Carol had a good head for figures.

She worked as a futures analyst in the City and could certainly handle very fast maths. She was way ahead in this game which meant she was even-stevens against Matt who worked for a rival firm. These past months they had played thirty-eight games and this one would put her ahead again. Ba-boom. Ten points, final game. Triumphant, she scythed the air with her Kevlar racquet. Then the two of them pretty much collapsed, slumping in the back of the court. Lungs heaving like bellows, they felt so, well, *oxygenated*. Carol had brought along a rare vintage of Chateau des Tours which they drank from paper cups, sweat falling like raindrops into the exquisite wine.

After showering they headed for their favourite café bar, where they both ordered espresso martinis, specifying both the coffee beans and the make of vodka. Money gave you choice.

Then Matt asked a rather unexpected question...

'I wonder what it's like to grow old?'

He raised an eyebrow in the direction of an old man who had just wandered in. He was hunchbacked by age and every movement rickety. His skin, on the other hand, had the colouration of someone who lived in the open air, stained like old teabags by wind and sun.

'Funny you should ask that,' said Carol, cradling her drink in her perfectly manicured hands. 'The company's taking us to this place next week where we're going to find out just that.'

'Just what?'

'What it's like to grow old.'

'You're kidding me.'

'When did I ever kid anyone?' Carol replied. Even conversation was a competition for her. She had to win at all things. Be the smartest. Be the fittest. Be the best performing futures analyst in the developed world.

Across the way the old man slurped tea from a saucer.

'How does that work?' continued Matt. 'This ageing thing?'

'I have no idea but my boss thought it would be really useful what with the sort of stuff I'm horse-trading at the moment.'

Carol spent her workdays speculating about probable investments in health care twenty years down the line, when the ageing explosion had turned into a supernova. You could make a fortune if you had all your ducks in a row.

Dentures.

Stair-lifts.

Mobility scooters.

Heck, in South Korea women were living to ninety. On average! To ninety years of age! That might be three or four new sets of false teeth in a lifetime. Grey change was certainly where it was at.

'I wonder what the scam is,' pondered Matt with a wry grin. 'Maybe they've cracked the secret of time travel. You'll visit the future in an old police box. First class on Tardis. Should be quite a ride.'

'I don't think it is a scam, Mark. I think they're on the level. This is a scientific establishment. A not for profit. '

'I'm sure it is. I guess I won't see you for a workout next week then. Maybe the week after?'

Carol said she'd see him if she wasn't feeling too old, which made them both laugh.

After she left Matt found himself regretting that he hadn't invited himself along. Whatever the con it had to be better than betting millions of pounds on the possibility of monsoons washing away tea plantations in the Indian hill country. His work wasn't boring but it was always tinged with disaster.

*

The Grey Havens was a 1930s building, all curved lines and balcony rails that made it look like a cruise liner, an impression deepened by the fog that wisped across the lawns. It seemed like a place custom designed for people cut adrift, loosed from their moorings.

The receptionist took more details than Carol expected – asking for various samples and asking her to demonstrate her lung capacity by blowing into a calibrated cardboard tube. She took a huge draught of air and blew into it like a veteran trombone player so that the receptionist almost clapped at how far the measuring line had moved. Carol was then told to follow Barry, an old retainer with a face like a prune.

She quickly inspected her room before settling in. There were signs on the walls, in the bathroom, pretty much everywhere, although the writing on all of them was at best indistinct. She struggled to make out the meaning of any of them.

Carol had been told there'd be a fitting at six o'clock sharp but not what the fitting was for exactly so she quickly showered.

At five minutes to the hour Carol wandered down to the wing called Autumn Royal. As she walked she tried to guess things about her fellow travellers who formed a nervous little procession but everyone was quiet, offering precious few clues.

Accompanying her as she walked was a voice very much like Ian McKellan's that drifted from speakers discreetly arranged in the corridor, its timbre and depth all velvet nicotine.

And you shall all come to the Grey Havens, eventually, when life's wind no longer plumps the sails, and the skeletal rigging creaks as do your old bones. Those old and weary bones made crumbly and dusty by osteoporosis.

Carol reckoned there was enough money in care homes for it to actually be Sir Ian. The Havens could afford to hire him. It would be a nice touch as there was something so very rich and comforting in his voice.

For at the Havens, at this sweet anchorage...

Lie empty vessels...

The broken hulls, the stranded ships, their crews all gone a-wandering.

In the main hall, called the Elli suite, after the Norse god of ageing, the latest batch of visitors to the Grey Havens were briskly divided into three groups – those who wore spectacles, those who wore contact lenses and those who wore neither. The lens wearers were fitted with replacement pairs, the lenses themselves scratched and opaque, while the specs were exchanged for ones that had really been through the wars, the glass seemingly sandblasted into fuzziness.

'Don't worry too much about the fit,' volunteered the optometrist, 'you'll all be wearing lenses by the weekend. Now we need to crack on...' He launched into a terse little lecture that quickly made the listeners feel frail and vulnerable.

'Let me tell you about Age, my friends. Your sense of touch will probably decrease, as will your ability to hear some high-pitched sounds. It's particularly noticeable in some men who may not be able to hear higher registers. There's a little bird called the grasshopper warbler, has a song like a fishing reel. A shy bird, mind. Well, I've known men in their sixties who can see the little bird's beak open as it trills but can't actually hear the notes it produces. Some smells might evade you and there's a loss of some of the sweet and salty taste buds. And then there are the eyes, my specialism...'

The man cued up a series of images on a screen. Carol winced inside. This was the reason she couldn't stand King Lear. 'All those eyes,' she thought. 'They drill right into my phobia...' She couldn't stand images of eyes.

The man continued, relishing the power of knowledge as he cued up every slide in turn.

'The lenses of your eyes lose some of their ability to accommodate, so you may find yourself reading at arm's length. The size of the pupil also decreases, possibly making it harder to adapt to dim light. You'll all know something about the eye and its deteriorations...'

Carol could barely look at the images through the fence of fingers she held up in front of her. 'Glaucoma.' 'Cataracts.' 'Straightforward blindness.' Oh dear.

'... These are the sorts of things that may affect you. Maybe one day you'll be checking in to a hotel room when you realize that the signs aren't that clear... that you're struggling to read them...'

Everyone in the room remembered the signs in their own rooms and an edgy nervousness set in, setting loose a fluttering of butterflies in people's stomachs.

'And although there isn't a direct correlation with what happens to sight the hearing is often affected at one and the same time...

'So by way of practical demonstration I'd you'd like to get a pair of . scissors each out of the box and then a couple of newspapers. I'd like you to cut out a series of squares about so big...'

He held up six-inch squares of paper. When they had each made a dozen or so squares he stapled them together and then showed how to set them in place over the ears, like the crudest possible earmuffs. They all looked ridiculous and they would have laughed as a gang at the sight of themselves were it not for the collective agitation of the nervy butterflies, which had grown bigger wings, some of them metallic, and were making people shudder inside. The facts about ageing seemed like an onslaught. Hearing loss was awful, even just this muffled effect, this turning down of the volume.

Later that evening Carol sat in the lounge for some cosmetic procedures. A woman from somewhere in south east Asia painted fake liver spots on the backs of her hands while another applied 'just a mild acid that will make your skin crinkle. It will all disappear after a couple of weeks as you shed your skin. Don't worry.' Don't worry, indeed! They also applied some dye to her limbs so that they changed to the colour of old parchment. It was quietly disarming.

As Carol sat there seeing her skin age various people came in to talk to her and it was as if they couldn't see she had wads of newspaper clamped over her ears. All she could see was their mouths opening and closing so that she felt like a goldfish in a bowl, the human faces beyond the glass as big as cinema screens.

Meanwhile in the corridor the voice so much like Ian McKellan's was talking as if to itself:

Life is, and always will tend towards shipwreck.

Wrecked thus, you shall drift into the Grey Havens, when the winds are gone from the sails and rigging, when the anchor's just a discard on some deep sea bed. When the whipping tempests of work and strife and rocky marriage have finally calmed.

In her room later that night Carol lay on the bed wearing her new, old spectacles. There was something vaguely comforting about not having to remember things, of being mollycoddled. Usually she had so much to analyse but here she could drift away from the barrage of news and streaming documents.

She stared up at the out-of-focus ceiling, recalling her mother's troubled journey into night. Early onset dementia had soon turned into total onset, or maybe assault as her mother was veritably besieged by symptoms of brain decay...

Forgetfulness.
Confusion.
Trouble with names.
Trouble with facts.
Almighty creakiness.
And more intimate matters, involving the plumbing, that quietly stole away her dignity.

Carol drifted.

Be still here.

Enjoy the deep serenity of the Havens. Rest your weary bones awhile.

For this is your Sargasso and in this sea you shall be lost, in the mysterious, glorious Bermuda triangle of senility, all adrift and all alone on the fathomless and all consuming sea, its drifting waves of age.

It was her mother's loss of language that had most upset her, though. It did nothing less than scare the Bejezus out of her. Her mother had always been a loquacious lady if nothing else, articulate to a fault. Carol would recall her using language as would a chef, careful about the ingredients, melding them into tasteful, poised sentences.

For her mother the plague of forgetfulness had started innocently enough, if a little stealthily – just the occasional lost word placed just out of reach of memory's fingers – microwave, aubergine, kettle – the last of which was most surprising given how much tea she drank.

But then her mother had started to drop phrases, or jumble up the grammar so that within six months what had been a rare consommé of elegant expression was all crazy gloops of minestrone, bits of this, bits of that all mixed in. She scrambled syllables or idiot words. 'Wunga,' she'd say. 'Wunga, wunga, wunga,' and Carol didn't have an earthly about what she wanted or what she was trying to say. She would stand there, helplessly, at the side of her mother's bed. It was as if the old gal was scaling the great cliff of miscommunication. Selfishly she worried about the possibility of her mother's condition being contagious or, worse still, congenital. Was this her future too, this dismantling decay?

Senility. Dangling on the Cliff of Fear the wild-eyed woman got her climbing gear all twisted up, the carabiners unclipped and the ropes all messed around her shoulders, steadily tying herself in knots of panic. Unsafe, above the irresistible verticality of the cliff face, Carol's mother drifted ever downward.

'Wunga, wunga, wunga,' she incanted as she dropped away into chasmic space.

Carol's mother was thrown back, by the irony of things, into the echo-chamber of unutterable silence.

The next morning, opaque spectacles on, Carol strained to see the other members of the group. They were just fuzzy figures arranged around the out-of-focus breakfast table.

'We'll be speeding up the pace of change in the next two days,' a new doctor said, pointing at some diagrams which no-one could see properly. 'We'll be filling up your ear canals with pats of jelly, all entirely biodegradable, shouldn't clog things up for more than a few days.'

He held up a tube of something, though people could only see the colour of it, a reassuring buttercup yellow. They all strained to make out the words on the label.

'The hearing will come back but we will also need to complicate your ability to move. We'll give you a proper sense of what happens when the arthritis kicks in, or clicks in – sorry that was a very weak sort of joke – and when the muscles aren't as taut. There tends to be a gradual loss of muscle tone, elasticity and strength.'

As the doctor unrolled his long list of predictions Carol found she had lost interest in her croissant.

' In some areas,' the doctor continued, 'the muscle is often replaced with fatty tissue leaving you with little rolls or flabby spots. Sadly, your endurance or strength to perform certain tasks may also decrease. Whereas in your youth you might have been able to run marathons or pulverize your bodies on a squash court when you enter the decline even climbing up a couple of steps can be like scaling Kanchenjunga. It can really take it out of you.'

Members of his audience struggled with the word. Cancha-what?

'Also the skeletal system gradually becomes more porous and brittle, as the bones lose calcium and their density. This may be more pronounced in women. As a result, you'll be prone to fractures, notice a decrease in height or even develop a stoop in your posture. So we'll be giving you a little foretaste of that, too. You'll have just a day of it, anything beyond that would be torture and I'd be in danger of being struck off.'

As the doctor said all this teams of assistants were putting all manner of strings and pulleys in place, clipping things on, tightening, adjusting the torque, the force that could make something turn on its axis. An elbow maybe. Reducing the torque reduced its mobility.

Carol smiled at the old man next to her – even though he was, in truth only twenty four – as they were both fitted with the various paraphernalia.

'I'm Peter,' he said as the weights pulled his body into a largely foetal shape.

'Carol,' answered Carol who already felt as if she was an inch shorter. When she got up to shake Peter's hand her feet dragged heavily as they crossed the floor, and the best she could manage was a kind of foolish amble.

Meanwhile, Peter, on the bed next to her, was given a more testing example of future detriment and deterioration. His back was bent into an arrow bow by strings of unyielding plastic that bound him into the sort of painfully awkward position that even a masochistic contortionist would avoid. The man who tied him into place had the bulk of a Sumo wrestler, so when he tied the knots they seemed tied for ever.

Strapped and bound and with the array of various weights in place pulling down on her, Carol found herself caught in an unexpected reverie as she remembered her father. He'd been a quiet hero, not least after the tragic accident at Puddy's factory when a loose bit of sleeve had dragged his arm into the meat slicer, cleaving it in two, half way between the wrist and elbow. It was quite un-saveable despite an emergency helicopter airlift and a twenty-two hour operation. But he had been brave and Carol realized she needed to draw on the sorts of reserves of strength her father had. Age was a scary continent to cross.

After the accident her father kept on doing what he'd always done. He went back to work at the same machines and in the evening still played jazz, with just his five fingers and he didn't change the music, still pounding out the same beloved jazz syncopations. Cab Calloway numbers, as if freshly minted at Harlem's Cotton Club, his thumb acting like a double bass, beating time like a marching band. Carol remembered how the old man had tried to stave off the effects of the dementia by studying Greek and algebra and chess tactics, and trying to learn all of Shakespeare by heart. As his condition got worse so did the late night recitations, the Bard's sonnets sounding increasingly dislocated and the characters straying from play to play, so that Hamlet fell in love with Bottom and a dark hearted Othello sang a mournful hey nonny no.

Carol found it hard to converse with anyone at supper what with her eyesight spotting mirages and the fact that she was finding it hard to lift any eating utensils with her weakened arms. She didn't like sucking soup through a straw but this was not a time for vanity. A smiling nurse tied a plastic bib around her neck. It had some creature on it.

'It's Daffy Duck,' Peter helpfully said. 'I didn't have you down as a Daffy fan.'

Carol sucked up her soup sarcastically, dragging the fluid into her mouth in such a way as to make the maximum noise. It was a small act entirely out of keeping with her character and disposition.

'I'll support any cartoon animal I please,' she said, defiantly stroking Daffy's head with a finger, which in itself was as much movement as the straps and weights allowed.

And in the Havens you shall rest. Throw overboard the burdensome cargo of worry so that it is just flotsam, jetsam, sea-wrack. Set yourself free from the troubling weight of memory, all those things you always felt you had to remember, the birthdays, shopping lists, the numbers for the credit cards, the phones.

Drift on my friends. That's it. Let the waves of age take you ever on and on. A drifting. That's what it is. A pleasant drifting, going hence to who knows where. On and on and on...

That night they held a social activity, a tea-dance for the 'old folks' at the Havens and Carol found herself spending a lot of time with Peter. By the time a Vera Lynn song had come around for the third time she was holding hands with him and after a couple of hours had elapsed she was venturing onto the dance floor, depending on him to hold her up now that some principal muscle groups had weakened to the point where they were already useless.

On the dance floor they moved in unexpected consort, their timing in unison despite the physical awkwardness. One step. Two steps... Three, four and turn.

Under the revolving disco lights Carol could discern the liver spots painted on the back of hands which had the pattern of islands against the ancient parchment tones of her skin. Her hearing was returning, so the music became something more than just a rhythm.

Peter was smiling, flashing his new-found dentures as if they made him look like George Clooney and just as attractive.

They went once more around, stumbling and hobbled, but still dancing after a fashion, in sweet and unexpected companionship.

Then the music stopped and Carol found herself staring into Peter's eyes, far more deeply than could be explained by the defective lenses she was wearing.

'Let's stay here awhile, in the Havens I mean. It's, well, strangely comforting.'

'And it's porridge for breakfast,' said Peter, adjusting his top set of dentures with hands that couldn't quite reach because of the plastic binds.

'Slurping heaven,' suggested Carol.

'We'll need our bibs,' Peter replied. 'Yours is a lemon colour as I recall.'

The fact that he had noticed the colour made Carol feel all warm inside. This old man was a soul mate, he really was. She knew she'd only just met him but she also felt she had known him forever.

As so they shuffled off to bed, their walking speed now slower than a snail's glide and each step was hard, a bit of rheumatic ordeal.

Carol and her new and ancient love were both walking and drifting. In her head she heard the refrains of very distant piano music, played by a man with only five fingers, defiant melodies coming at her from years gone by.

She knew they were almost there.

Their bedrooms were only a few miles further. Maybe she would invite him in.

Just a few long miles to go.

Class Ghost

The Tuesday night menu in the refectory was always the worst, food so vile and indigestible that it would be referred to as 'The slop' or the 'Gloop of doom' by the boys, their eyes ablaze with hunger. But not so much hunger that they could face the bowls of execrable gruel. This particular Tuesday was worse, being the last Tuesday before Christmas and matron's brother in law Swem had been emptying the traps by the canal so that the bowls were a minestrone of amphibian and culvert-dwelling mammal. Fourth-former Terrence Beech turned green after a spoonful and had to excuse himself to go outside. And was never seen again.

The upper forms spent the night combing the woods for him, their lanterns and school-issue cowls making them look like processionals of monks attending very late vespers among the conifers. They found a badger carcass and signs of some villagers indulging in black magic but not a trace of Beech other than for a stand of trees of the same name. It was as if he had photosynthesised.

Now Terrence Beech wasn't one of the most popular pupils in the school but that didn't mean that his fellow pupils, known as 'sufferers' didn't feel some shreds of anxiety at his disappearance. Some even volunteered to make up a search party but were told in no uncertain terms that the police had it all under control as evidenced by the number of Alsatians coming out of a fleet of vans, augmented by Scrote the gardener's elderly bloodhound Boris, which knew that manhunt meant reward and was happy to get his nose to ground for a while in order to earn some chocolate buttons.

The school reacted strangely to the disappearance as you'd expect: it was a weird place, a mix of Dotheboys Hall and San Quentin. A normal establishment would have cancelled the carol concert but Hardwick Boys' Correctional decided to go on with the show. They got the choir to make and wear masks based on the photograph of Beech which was being used by the police and the media so that they were all identikit and exceedingly spooky. It was like some strange Yuletide production of a Greek tragedy, the chorus all back from the dead.

In the general science lesson the next afternoon Form Five were presented with the sight of the science master Mr Bowles standing in front of the class along with the chaplain.

'Now then boys. I've asked the Reverend Smythe along as our experiment today will try to ascertain the weight of the soul. It's been said that it weighs exactly twenty one grammes... some of you may have seen the film of the same name and in light of what happened to young Beech I thought it might be appropriate to not only conduct the experiment but also to consider the not insignificant matter of the soul. I'll hand over to you now if I may Mr Chambers?'

The chaplain was an owl faced squinter of a man, whose short-sightedness was only one of his legion problems. He had body odour that could wrestle one to the ground, the sort of crippling aroma that would surely be of interest to scientists as a military option. His oratory, however, was top shelf.

'The soul, that vital spark is one of the deepest Christian mysteries and I use those last two words most advisedly. As Alexander Pope said in his probing poem:

> *Vital spark of heav'nly flame!*
> *Quit, O quit this mortal frame:*
> *Trembling, hoping, ling'ring, flying,*
> *O the pain, the bliss of dying!*
> *Cease, fond Nature, cease thy strife,*
> *And let me languish into life.*

'That oxymoron, pain mixed with bliss is perhaps what happens when he shrugs off the carapace of the mortal frame and ascends, yes ascends as many of us surely must to the great open reaches of heaven, to the angel fields, where the trumpets shall sound to welcome the righteous who shall indeed languish into life, the new life, the life reborn as the soul shines for all eternity. Personally I laugh at the idea of the soul having a specific weight but I hope my little, well flight of rhetoric gives you some context for the science inquiry you're about to conduct. And don't forget you'll all be welcome in chapel on Christmas Day. Seven o'clock sharp. Bring your best voices.'

'Thank you, chaplain,' said Bowles with only a faint hint of sincerity. One might have got the impression that he'd only invited him along to cover his back, lest their experiment have unexpected or even uncontrollable consequences. As it happened only the two brightest members of the class managed to get any valid data, managing to prove that the weight of the laboratory rat's soul was 1.8 grammes. They had weighed it before and after the gassing and there really was a difference, as if the chaplain's vital spark had density as well as energy. They wondered if Beech had a soul and if so how they might have weighed him in sufficient detail. Presuming he was dead of course, which many did as he'd been gone a few days now and the nights were perishing.

In the abomination known as double maths the following day the teacher, Mr Hastings was explaining some of the precepts of statistical analysis and chose to do so with a question that managed to chill the blood of some of the more nervous pupils.

'If there are 399 pupils in the hall for dinner and one of them goes missing – possibly for ever, possibly until his bleached bones, picked clean by the crows, are unearthed beneath a hedge – then what proportion of the student body is considered lost?'

In the maths class the silence was glacial, not only because the boys couldn't work out the sum in question but also because they didn't like the fact that Terrence Beech was being used as casually as a decimal point. It didn't seem to be in good taste, or even necessary.

They needn't have worried because in the following Thursday's double lesson Terrence made an appearance, sitting at his usual desk, surrounded by a silvery aura that glistened like a snail. He was silent, in keeping with the majority of ghostly apparitions but there was something fixed about his eyes, glazed like the icing on a doughnut, staring at Hastings as if he knew something about him, something bad. Which was indeed the case because Hastings was involved in the young boy's disappearance and that in a way that most people would scarcely believe.

Hastings had recently started an affair with a young girl in the village which had led to tensions and an incident involving a crossbow, not that those were directly involved with the Beech disappearance. But they made him nervy, especially as he was a man with a secret to hide, in being matron's brother and as a consequence drawn into a family spiral with her brother in law, the hunter and trapper. It was he who'd first mooted the idea of making and setting a mantrap to catch the peeping tom who'd been sighted three times in the past week. Hastings thought it was an extreme reaction to a sad pervert, hidden in the privet bushes outside the gym and once seen slinking past the croquet lawn wearing what someone swore was an actual mackintosh. But they made the trap, with jaws made from triangles of steel manufactured in the metalwork class and a spring mechanism that had been rescued from an old locomotive, a powerful arrangement that clamped shut the mouth of the trap in the blink of a bat's eye.

It caught Beech rather than the peeping tom, pretty much took off his legs below the knee and Hastings and Swem had to put him out of his misery even as a boy soprano sang *The Holly and the Ivy* in the refectory, which helped muffle the sound of the claw hammer blow which put a bleak, precise hole in the boy's forehead, dispatching him like a trout.

They disposed of the body in an adit leading into a disused coal mine and once they'd finished that foul deed Swem laid down a network of false scents and trails presuming there'd be dogs involved in looking for the boy. He dropped pieces of blood pudding in patches of leaf litter, scattered drifts of bone marrow he would normally use on the tomatoes on paths and driveways. And that might have been it, other than for the Dostoyevskian trouble for their consciences. But Beech came back, haunting Hastings in every waking hour and walking into his sleep as well. The teacher lost interest in eating, picking like a wren at a mince pie.

And lessons were adapted to reflect the mystery of the schoolboy plucked from the woods and his ghostly manifestation, the way he turned up to stare and stare. In English they studied passages from a book called *Possession: the Uses of Haunting in the Hudson Valley* which showed how various American ghost stories changed and mutated over time.

Some days dead boy Beech would be there for all the science lessons of the day, his very existence flying in the face of the empirical and thwarting the validity of experiment. Hastings grew thinner, more vexed with every passing hour, while Swem the hunter and trapper could not go outside without Terrence coming as silent witness to any of his actions. It was beyond disconcerting, so Swem started to drink heavily, at all hours, hoping to banish the spectral fifteen-year-old via rivulets of booze. The boy, meanwhile, now lived in a realm far beyond science – though a place, in truth, without a single angel or trace of heaven. And he would haunt his murderers diligently, even on Christmas Day, sitting just beyond the plates of pudding and leftover ham, staring with Antarctic eyes, ones that would never shut, eternal witnesses to his killers' dissolutions.

Sonata Envy

Smethwick knew in his marrow that it happened differently for them, the other composers, damn their ears. And how he cursed those hearing flaps: the small ones, furled tight like young bracken and the ones that looked like seashells of pink icing: then the big flaps like elephants. Bruckner's were like that. He was his nemesis, not that any of the others were his friends.

Let the gods of all music make sure they all woke up one morning with those finely-attuned organs of theirs totally and terminally gummed up. Let there be some infectious yellow marmalade clogging the canals of the inner ear, a thick gunk suffocating the cochlea. Gooseberry jam, thick as mucus, rich with irritating seeds at the end of the Eustachian tubes. Let Walton's head be full of muffle. And Elgar's while you're at it. And Bartok and Beethoven and Mahler and the whole bally lot, damn their shades. Cursed as they were with talent.

They – Strauss, Ligeti, Hoddinott and that Vaughan bloody Williams – were his competitors, all the dead ones and the live ones, those who conjured perfect sounds to take your breath away, or ran a line of song so fine, so, well transcendent that he would quiver with envy when he heard the melodies and harmonies, the euphonious conjunctions and ecstatic violins. He'd shake his stick at them if he had one.

They seemed to mock him, both the dead and practising. Mocking him, Peter Smethwick, a very minor composer from Walberswick, Suffolk whose entire work and effort was only worth only four lines in *Groves' Dictionary*. He had only ever garnered a couple of trivial prizes and produced one work deemed worthy of an outing at the Proms. That lasted just over four minutes and had been reviewed by some cloth-eared turd who dismissed it as a 'prentice bagatelle' in the *Telegraph*. He had a little bit of trifling telly music to his name, too. He'd penned the theme tune to a series about the last milkmen in Yorkshire - with a very fine trumpet voluntary which evoked sparkling tarns and becks cutting through limestone, and some incidental music for a food programme presented by a man with a head like a turnip. Not much to show for a life.

Yes, the others mocked his pathetic efforts with the magic of their work.

There was that passage for example in Sibelius Five that almost brought on an asthma bout, so beautifully wrought was it, so terrifyingly authentic and lush with import. Sometimes he didn't know why he bothered to try to explain in words what that melody did to him. It was all quite simply beyond words, and explication. There was one thing for certain: it made him want to hang up his fiddle, to bonfire his piles of pristine manuscript paper and watch them burn into grey confetti. And then again there was Warlock's *The Curlew* with the sound of wind susurrating through the reeds and the plangent sound of the heart's emptiness, not to mention the curlew itself, flying through each gorgeous passage as if over a silvered river. How did he do that? Where did that *hauntingness* come from? Warlock was a wonder, sure as eggs is eggs. Not to mention Bartok. Now he could murder him with his bare hands. If he wasn't dead already.

How he hated those other composers who had it so damned easy, their sonatas and cadenzas and soaring flights of melody coming to them almost unbidden, while he had to slave over a hot stave. All right, that wasn't the best of puns but he was tired, so atrociously depleted. And he blamed them! All they had to do was wait patiently in their oak-lined studies or in those ornate high-ceilinged offices in the elegant conservatoires of Europe and the notes would eventually migrate towards them, settling like swallows on a wire – jittery, yes, perhaps a tad restless, but ultimately regimented there, all in place, their forked tail feathers pointing down the bottom of the stave. All they had to do was wait. For those serried ranks of birds on wires, the signal birds of inspiration.

For him it was long, hard graft and hours and hours and hours of waiting, often to little end and thinnest purpose. The random, long-sought after notes first appeared as clouds of shocked birds, a confusion, a murder of ravens just hurled into space by the sound of a shotgun shot and stopped in their tracks as they tore out the jellied eyes of a dead lamb. Smethwick would have to make sense of those black shapes, wrench them into place. As if they'd ever truly settle. Not now anyway, with their dagger-bills trailing death slime, red as pyrites. They, the fortunate composers, had wheeling swallows and he had blood-kissed ravens. Go figure.

Yet, on a good day, when the muse arrived all calm and tranquil, his melody was clear to hear, there in the sorcelling song of his own curlew, rising high over the peat fields and the sharp spikes of rush and bog grass. Then he need only transcribe, his notes sitting patiently as they did for the others, like neat hirundines on tightened lines, all strung taut with potential.

And on blessed days such as those he would well nigh choke on the beauty of what he heard, the fluid ascendancy of the notes as they took the imagined flute solo higher, the breathtakingness of the move from his inner ear through the marked page to the confident musician's quite faultless execution. What he wrote in this, the chill of his cottage, in the cold that made his very blood turgid and his frame almost rigid, another human being would play on a stage with hundreds listening and if they liked the vibrations in the inner ear then how rapturous would be the applause, what air-vibrations then? What miracle this! What rare creation!

He so envied the others, though. He'd happily pay someone to horsewhip the pathetic hides of his contemporaries, of Bullstrode and Heidrich Wire and that Wagnerian bully Masterson, well, wouldn't it be just the thing if a slinky psychopath, adept with piano wire, could visit him as he slept in that pretentious island lighthouse of his? Garotte him gently as he slept. It would be doing him, and the world of music an undying favour. Atonal nonsense! The scraping of nails on a blackboard. Pah!

Smethwick's envy was unbecoming, he knew, unbecoming and ultimately caustic, gnawing away at the pillars of his soul, making an empty cave of him.

But he had so much to contend with, having to make sense of the wild raven flocks, as they flapped maraudingly through his mind.

Or musical notes that came courtesy of Stuka fighter aircraft, slaloming through the air with their chat-chat-chattering machine guns, bullets ripping through his cortex so that it ended up resembling a cabbage stalk gnawed by rats, the sort his gardening uncle Foster left to rot in the winter-patch. Notes in attack formation, take-no-prisoner-squadrons out to shoot the hell out of his grey matter.

Mechanical screams in the air. The music of incipient madness.

They never had Nazi fighters flying into their heads. He was damn sure of that. Although Shostakovich, it must be said, did have some attack squadrons of his own to deal with. Plenty of death in the air for Dmitri.

Sweet Jesus! He'd just remembered who was coming today. Today was the day that Albert Mostyn was coming for tea and he wasn't the sort to be satisfied with just a basic scone and a blob of clotted cream no matter how delicious. He'd be wanting fancy cakes presented on lace doilies and tea made in a silver samovar and Smethwick just knew that today he didn't so much as have the makings of even the lowliest cup of char. Hell's teeth, this was as inconvenient as a pull of the dropsy. Where would he get elegant cakes, the sort of things Albert could nibble with those ridiculous rabbit teeth of his? Lord, the last time he'd gone to see John the baker down in Aldeburgh and asked whether he had anything with currants in he'd looked at him strangely. Currants for Pete's sake! The old man looked at him as he was were asking for a dusting of manna.

Today, of all days to have forgotten that his fellow composer was arriving after a gargantuan and unassailably uncomfortable journey. He started his preparations, sifting some flour and breaking four eggs...

Unbeknown to the two men their lives were to be forever altered by a meeting that very afternoon in Sweden. In grand rooms in Stockholm assistants danced a practised waltz around mahogany tables, depositing heavy paperwork as if it were eiderdown. A winter sun, reflected from chill harboursides, gave the seated men's skulls a watery sheen. High cranial lobes made out of granite, eyes chiselled into place between haughty temples. Men dressed in black, funereal black, as if they were going to bury one another. They were men who made money from war, which they spent on aquavit. The meeting was handed over to Hendrick Nobel, great great grandson of the famous chemist.

Hendrick was a musician, himself of no great promise, but it was nevertheless a crazy passion of his and so he wanted to create the largest music prize ever. The committee was being asked to ratify his request, even though it would create a prize worth ten times the value of the science award instigated by his distinguished relative. Would it not suggest that music was somehow superior to science, to chemistry in particular, seeing as that was what made Alfred's name, not to mention his millions of kroner. Surely Alfred would turn in his lead-lined grave?

Debate was brisk and focussed on the inevitability of classical music winning the day. Hendrick was adamant that it wasn't absolutely necessary that classical music had to win the day. The rules allowed for folk song, tunes for marching bands, even national anthems. The gentlemen in the room, though world wearied and deeply cynical in the main could see how this would generate debate and deepen the world's respect for Nobel and his largesse. Which explains why, when the case was made for the humongous prize that there was no dissent. Rather there was a silent show of hands, and then Sturm, who was always the wag, whistled a little shepherd's song which they'd all learned as children and suggested that it would be a contender. They all laughed, and the officers in the next room were astonished to hear a chorus of whistling coming through the walls, complete with peals of laughter. In fact they recognized the tune and couldn't for the life of them work out why the Nobel prize committee should be piping up with it, and doing so with such gusto.

Smethwick was washing dishes after Mostyn's dismal visit and listening to the *PM* programme on Radio 4 when he heard about the prize, becoming well-nigh apoplectic with excitement. Then reality kicked in when he remembered the legions, or at least the dozens of composers whose music was much better. Surely they would win the prize and leave him floundering in the shallows.

And then the phone rang. It was his old music tutor, Dr Jenner from the Royal Holloway, with a strange bit of information. Jenner spoke in a stage whisper, even though he was on the telephone...

'I know you to be an envious old crow and I'm sure news of this prize will have more than whetted your appetite, so I'd like to make an introduction for you.'

'An introduction, you say. What sort of introduction, and to whom?'

'Let's just say someone who will be able to make winning all that money more of a possibility.'

'Do you mean you know one of the judges? That would be somewhat underhand would it not? A tad irregular...'

'No,' said Dr Jenner, his voice heavy with mystery. 'It's just someone who takes care of things. I just have to ask you one question and that in deadly earnestness. How far would you go to be the best living composer in Britain?'

'Oh I think I can say I would be prepared to go all the way. Yes, indubitably. All the way. Whatever it takes.'

'I surmised that was the sort of length...'

Peter Smethwick met Harold Weobley the following Friday. He looked quite ordinary. Apart from the eyes. They belonged to an eagle or a falcon. Hyper-alert. All-seeing. And predatory.

The most efficient assassin in Western Europe was practising his hand movements, the sharp, vertebrae-snapping twist of a garotte, the wire deft and taut between his practised hands. This was how he dispatched that Italian composer once, who thought he was safe because the ferry was within sight of the white cliffs of Dover. But he hadn't bargained with meeting Weobley in the conveniences, or having the life throttled out of him even as the lights of English buoys – marking the closing approach to harbour – sent weak flares of light against the ship's sides. Almost there, but not quite. Weobley stashed his victim in one of the lifeboats, loving the irony of that. A lifeboat! For the cadaver. Exquisite.

So the man sitting opposite Smethwick in the Little Chef, the calculating killer with the accipitrine eyes was Harold Weobley, the veritable doyen of assassins who specialized in killing composers. His father'd done the same before him and even his grandfather was known to dabble. Think that Webern died because of an Allied bullet? Think again.

Weobley was the subject of musical urban tales and nightmares among the string section. No-one knew what he looked like so people imagined the worst. One eye. A Machiavellian sneer. Sabre scarred cheeks like a pantomime duellist. A face with no features. He could be what you wanted him to be. But for now he had to strengthen his fingers because the last time he had to get up close to his victim he almost failed to squeeze the last breath out of his lungs as his fingers grew tired even as the strangulated man's visage turned puce then blackberry then the black of ripe sloes. There was only one man who knew his true identity: Dr Jenner knew about his 'work' as he liked to call it, and that because he was a friend of Weobley's father and had paid him to dispatch an academic rival who happened to be the organ scholar at Magdalene.

They talked about the catalogue of victims, established how easy it would be to find out things about their daily routines. Then the two men agreed terms. Fifty thousand pounds – his life savings – for getting the rivals out of the way and then twenty per cent should he gain the grand prize. They did not shake hands. Weobley was ultra careful with his DNA.

And so he set about his grim reaping, working his way through the list. He poisoned the first, an *avant garde* practitioner from Marseilles on the night of the premiere of his latest chamber opera based on one of Alice Hoffman's stories, using lethal tinctures brewed from houseplants. They were well nigh untraceable and the police labs never thought to look for such seemingly innocuous stuff as the juice of Swiss cheese plants or the deadly sap of moonflower with its atropine, its hyoscine, and well nigh untraceable hyoscyamine. Weobley spent a busy night wandering through the conservatory harvesting the roots of kaffir lily, which he would boil down and boil down until what might have been just a source of irritation turned into something much, much worse. Three tiny drops of it and you were a goner.

The poor man didn't see it coming, the little dart made from rush stems hitting the neck from the perfectly aimed blowpipe. Weobley made sure he saw the man brush away the evidence and walked briskly out of his hiding place behind the Wigmore Hall service ramp. Had someone seen him they'd have said that he seemed to turn into mist, shimmer into nothingness like someone teleporting in *Star Trek*.

By the time he'd dispatched the next two best British composers – Maxwell Williams and Morton Keppler – the papers had picked up on it, noting the devilish pattern that was emerging. The *Daily Mail* tagged him 'The Musical Murderer' which seemed quite benign, charming and chiming, not really a Ripper, not as chill as, say a 'Moors Murderer.'

As hysteria ramped up, some of the remaining composers started to employ bodyguards and even the most obscure minimalist installed better home security, with arc lamps and alarm systems that triggered rapid police response. Tension spread. Fear took hold. There were the first instances of first nights being cancelled because of jitteriness and the Proms season saw its audiences dwindle.

But Weobley was up to the job, and loved nothing better than a challenge and if it happened to be mission impossible then he was truly in his element. The fact that the musical community was on tenterhooks, on tiptoe with terror was just a spur to further action. And in an act of remarkable chutzpah he blew up Mostyn's house by remote control, having arranged for a delivery of very high explosive in a pizza box. That made the police completely aware that they were dealing with a total specialist, a professional who was faultless in his execution, with the emphasis on execution.

All this should have made Smethwick happy, but with every death he felt the very land grow ever more silent. He'd started something he couldn't control, and what made it worse was that he wasn't able to contact the Musical Murderer because once he'd made his payment, or 'creative investment' as Weobley put it, the killer was entirely incommunicado.

And so he sweated at nights and panicked by day, so vividly aware that he had started something awful which he couldn't now control, like the creator of a monster, or the inventor of a chemical weapon that was quite indiscriminate. He wanted nothing more than being able to get Weobley to stop and desist but he hadn't the foggiest how to get in touch with the killing machine. His old tutor didn't return his calls: he was hanging in the dressing room, been there for weeks.

One Monday came the news that Hector Wheatleigh had died in his sleep but because of the other deaths and the ensuing mayhem there had to be a particularly exhaustive post mortem which concluded that he had indeed just passed away peacefully and that there was no foul play to suspect.

Intuitively, Weobley then went to ground for a couple of months, then started to plan his next moves. The target was Hugh Mac, a rising star of the ECM label, a creator of glacial trumpet sounds evoking fjords plate-locked by ice and whose CDs were a staple of middle class dining parties as surely as Sigur Ros or *A Kind of Blue*.

Hugh Mac lived in a rented house on the edge of the university where he was composer in residence and believed himself to be sufficiently obscure that there was no danger whatsoever in his walking along the poplar-lined avenues between home and office. But Weobley had had the foresight to get a job there, working the boiler rooms and so bestowed with an outsize key ring giving him all the access he needed. So it was easy to arrange the sort of death that even the most diligent – hell's teeth, even the most visionary Scene of Crime team – would fail to recognize as any kind of crime at all. It would look like a simple accident, where Mac would simply have fallen back from his chair and banged his head against a radiator. The autopsy would suggest he had a pre-existing heart condition, without Weobley giving anyone a celluloid cat in hell's chance of guessing that someone had been adulterating the milk in the fridge next to Mr Mac's desk with tiny amounts of a chemical derived from a plant that only grew in full moonlight and only where certain hormones produced by pregnant anacondas seeped into the mud of the banks of an Amazonian tributary. It was the perfect crime. Weobley knew this in his bones.

But then things started to go awry, mainly because Weobley started to over-reach himself, and one would have to go as far as to suggest that he started to suffer from delusions of grandeur, or at the very least overblown ideas about his abilities, extraordinarily skillful but still not superhuman.

His key mistake was to broaden out his sphere of operations to include conductors as well as composers, kidnapping the maestro of the Birmingham Symphony mainly because he knew he could and then not really knowing what to do with him. He didn't feel the need to ask for a ransom and so he used him as a tool for scaring other composers, sending notes to the *Times* suggesting 'Lightning Will Strike Conductors' and indeed some of the more timorous among them did cancel engagements. The Sage in Newcastle put its celebration of John Adams on hold. Just to be on the safe side. Edinburgh's double bill of Satie and Ravel at the Usher Hall was cancelled because the pianist's fingers started to tremble uncontrollably.

Despite the stillness of the Suffolk night outside, with the air so, well, solid, a candle flame would burn straight upwards, Smethwick writhed, inasmuch as the chaise longue on which he lay allowed for writhing. He'd just read about Heidrich Wire's car accident, a bad smash that pulped him into raspberry jam near Junction 23 of the M6, knowing that this was Weobley's work, something involving a couple of snips of the brake lines late at night and then a little action-time roadwork in a white van to encourage the composer over the central reservation to meet his maker along with a lorry load of tulips just arrived from Rotterdam.

Meanwhile the net was closing on Weobley, gossamer threads tightening on the fly.

In the orchestra changing room of the Purcell rooms SWAT teams were donning Kevlar vests and checking their guns. They'd had a tip-off from a crystal ball gazing medium called Belle Epoque based in Brighton, who'd seen a murderer's hands holding a bill of fare for a concert of Schumann, Bruckner and Pierre Boulez – the very bill of fare for tonight's concert. Some of the attendants selling programmes were Special Branch. Undercover police officers outnumbered genuine punters seven to one.

They caught him like a bullfinch on a lime stick. Weobley was shocked at his own ineptitude, aghast that his radar for danger had performed so dully.

That night he had plenty of time to ponder his misdemeanours in the holding cell at Paddington Green, built to house IRA men and so withstand a Semtex blast.

As did Smethwick, his nerves settling, even as the titanic scale of the crimes he'd urged into being threatened to overwhelm him.

He knew what he'd done. They both knew what they'd done.

In the Albert Hall there was a cloying velvet hush. Only a solitary house mouse, acreep in the wainscoting made the tiniest claw clicks as it sought out crumbs of water biscuit.

In a symphony hall in Manchester the only sound was of dust settling, the thistledown of human skin forming the thinnest silver carpet on the serried ranks of chairs.

In the places of music making there was emptiness, the fallen echoes of ghost strings and saddened trombones.

Two men had done this. One with skill and one from envy.

Had silenced the joy of cadenza, replaced it with the hiss of fear.

Made each great hall a mausoleum, an echo chamber, a place of plush expectancy.

This they had done.

Made of each orchestra pit a leper colony.

Had left the music murdered in the aisles.

The
Full Treatment

'You want the Yorkston?' asked the man with ferocious tattoos. 'Nobody asks for that, not unless they don't want to live to see tea-time.' But I wanted it, that release, more than breath itself. My father'd been to this place, ten years previously, had had a full and apparently very satisfying Yorkston and then taken his place among the quiet dead. We'd actually picked up his body through the very door I'd just entered. They had phoned us with the news and stressed that he had died with a smile on his face.

'So, you want one even though you know what it entails. The full Yorkston. Certain?'

I nodded my complete assent.

'So, it's five thousand pounds, upfront. We only take cash.'

I counted out the twenties without so much as a hand tremor. By now the tattooed man could see I was deadly serious: there was that much to go on about my demeanour. I was wearing my poker face. On his arm a demon bird twitched its slate coloured primary feathers, as if readying for take-off.

'Very well, then. Take off your clothes. The Portabed is ready.'

I took my place among the other customers in what I can only describe as a cross between a TV studio and a sauna, with lots of theatre lights making all the flesh blemishes on the amplitude of flesh all too apparent. Some of the people lounging around in the steam haze looked like seals, others like walruses. They were all pretty fat and most of them seemed very happy.

I was told they'd call my name when my turn came, so I picked up two magazines – one to hide my private parts and the other to read – but neither offered me much in the way of reading pleasure. *Burning Rubber* was a bimonthly title about Formula 1 racing, which had never interested me although I once found my auntie Pat reading the biography of the racing car driver Stirling Moss. When I asked her why the interest she told me she wanted to learn how to drive faster. Having seen her nursing up the Hillman Imp to maybe twenty miles an hour I knew it would take more than this dog-eared biography to build up her speed. Thinking about her, and her sauntering driving around the village on a Sunday took my mind off the import of coming here. My father had come here to die. The walruses and seals in the sauna room had probably come here for the self-same reason. And I had no idea how it would happen, no earthly idea. Just that it would happen this afternoon. I had paid five thousand quid for the privilege and it was nearer than Switzerland, with its euthanasia clinics.

To kill time I read the other magazine that was full of pictures of debutantes with perfect teeth at fancy parties, standing next to Ruperts and Tituses, a kind of pornography for inbred rich kids. I started to indolently pick out the eyes from the photos with a hangnail.

When a man came in and announced himself as Theophilus Yorkston it caused, as you might expect, a sharp intake of breath.

'... But you can call me Mr Poland. Everyone else does. It's what my friends call me anyway, and we will be friends albeit only for a while.'

'Mr Poland?'

'It's a long story but I'll give you the digest. I used to work in Porton Down, in the government's experimental laboratories, where they trial all the latest chemical weapons. Oh we use them too you know. Anyway, I was the go-to-guy when it came to isotopes and it was natural for me to volunteer for one of the tests, which involved being subjected to gradually increasing doses of radiation. It took six weeks and I was given enough radiation to floor all the denizens of Donetsk. They all reckoned I should have died but my body seemed to keep on adapting, and soon they were talking about the process in terms of venom and anti-venom with everyone getting very excited in this the age of the dirty bomb and so on. So now I'm full to the core with polonium and yet I'm alive and no one really understands why. I am a curiosity, and scientists can't get enough of me.'

'But Mr Poland?'

'Polonium was so named because it was first discovered in Poland. Ergo Mr Poland.'

'I'm confused. My father came here for a Yorkston, which seems to be a way of dispatching someone, of helping them shuffle off this mortal coil and you're named Yorkston, yet now you're encouraging me to call you Mr Poland.'

'The Yorkston is indeed a method. Let's give you an example. Even though I'm fully able to live with the noxious effects of high level radiation any lover of mine, especially if we exchanged bodily fluids would be sure to die a fairly swift and sudden death.'

'Your lover?'

'Should you so choose. I know I'm not that attractive but you'd hardly feel a thing.'

'Surely there's another way. I'm sure my late father wasn't loved to death by you. Tell me he wasn't...'

'Correct.'

'So how was he, well, despatched.'

'That's too *sudden* a word. It was much gentler than that. As you'll find. Come with me...'

He held out a hand and took me into what he described as The Inner Sanctum. It had all the paraphernalia of a New Age quack – incense, whale music, bead curtains and paintings that could have been made by devotees of Timothy Leary back in the heyday of lysergic acid. Day-glo landscapes with arrays of coconuts palms and wide winged birds.

He told me to sit in the chair and offered me a cake. It was a piece of Battenburg and unbeknown to me it was laced with a super-efficient poison harvested from a snake that lives on the banks of the Orinoco.

As my organs seized I caught a glimpse of my father, kissing Mr Yorkston on those lips that could make a Geiger counter wail. So that's how he'd gone. A new experience to complement the one of dying. Worth five thousand quid however you looked at it. Then the aroma of patchouli wrapped itself around me and bore me aloft. The whales sang a song I almost recognised. It was a good dying, so, I beseech you, do start saving up. The Full Yorkston. That's what our family recommends.

Heskyn at Large

On the day of his release the Governor stared at Graham Heskyn for a long, hard while, scrutinising him from under steel eyelids, before saying he had never before entertained such a sick creature under the roof of his prison.

'You have shown no remorse whatsoever, and it pains me to have to send you back to society, knowing that you will probably strike again, like a Gabon pit viper.'

Heskyn thought the snake analogy a trifle over-wrought but decided not to spit any venom at the man, not now anyway. He knew where he lived, so he could answer the slight at some future time. Leafing through a file, Mr. Grisham reminded him that he would not be allowed to work with food ever again and that that was a strict condition of his probation. Fat chance, thought Heskyn-the-Poisoner, who had already circled an advert in the evening paper for a sous chef.

He walked out the prison gates and into a violet city, evening falling into indigo. It had been sixteen years since he'd first gone inside, and he was supposed to be in for life. So freedom was like an oxygen mask. And a reward. Heskyn had studiously played the good-boy card, kept mum, kept schtum and always volunteered to clean the toilets, even during The Outbreak as it was known when it was like the Nile in there. Whatever. It was a good ruse to stay out of the way of those who wished him harm, and there were many such folk. The Neath and Port Talbot chapter of the Aryan Brotherhood, for example, who smuggled in medical scalpels for their late-night torture sessions. Nasty to a fault, them. The McGuire twins, who made most rabid socio-paths seem like Mr Tumble. And the ferocious meat-hunters of E-block, who hated the world and wanted to proclaim that hatred as if sounding it with brass trumpets. They were determined cannibals, part of a morally putrid tribe. Ate Sunday lunch which was nothing short of terrifying, lips puckering over the ribboned evidence of the victim's last act.

Given the calibre of human monster he faced in prison it was just this side of a miracle that he managed to survive the years. But his mother helped him a lot – the ghost of his dead mother that is. Ever since his father had legged it to Scunthorpe she had been so very protective, held him close, breast fed him until he was almost six. She was the one who had introduced him to poisons.

Heskyn had been famous once, being the man who finished off an entire restaurant's worth of diners with his very tasty, creamy but deadly patisserie. The *Daily Mail* called him 'The Pastry Poisoner' and the moniker stuck. During the course of one ghastly evening he had served cyanide-laced choux buns to an old couple who had, in reality, only ordered a couple of grappas, not involuntary euthanasia. He also presented an Eton Mess to a family of four that was smothered with a topping of clotted cream and nerve agent. They ate it greedily until the father turned green and the rest of them followed suit, so that they looked like a Sickert painting as their bodies grew rigid and tinged with verdigris. He'd timed it so that he could have an espresso all by himself, before turning himself in. That had always been the plan, and he was nothing if not a stickler.

He thought it would be hard to find somewhere to stay but he'd been given the address of a dilapidated B&B which took in pretty much anyone and didn't ask questions. The old lady who ran the place was so old and arthritic that guests took it in turn to carry her down to the kitchen. She was a strange totem child in their arms, her hair hanging like wicker strands and the thin limbs made of dowelling poking out of her M&S haircloth dressing gown. Each and every morning she would be installed near the old range, croaking out orders about where things were kept and how many eggs to have on the go at any one time. Heskyn bided his time and waited his turn. To cook.

He got on with the old woman, who was called Mrs Flowers and had a truly marvellous array of prescription drugs to swallow every day. She'd been ill for a long, long time and had been prescribed a bit of this for pain relief, a bit of that for depression. All in all she took nineteen different kinds of pills and arrayed together they had a colour range to match the complete Jelly Bean collection, including the rare 'Mango and Sherbet', that collector's item.

'Help yourself,' she told him whenever he watched her popping the pills. Heskyn knew he shouldn't, what with his history of addictions, so he took only the purple tranquillisers and the ones in silver wraps, until Mrs Flowers pointed out they were suppositories, or for 'the other end' as she put it, laughing until her little bird-bones shook.

The morning dawned when it was Heskyn's turn to prepare breakfast and there happened to be an Irish road gang staying for a week and they truly did have trenchermen's appetites, as befitting men who actually did dig trenches. The old lady suggested cooking four rashers of bacon each, and using the two spare toasters to ensure supply met demand. Heskyn assessed the dining room, full of potential victims and patted his pocket and the two phials his cousin had obtained for him from Porton Down laboratories before the poor guy got caught by the Military Police and barred for life from working for the government. Heskyn didn't have the foggiest what was actually in the phials and even if it was chemical or biological, but the phials themselves, with their security lids and double vacuumed seals, suggested that whatever was inside was best kept inside. He patted them again, tenderly this time, as if they were furry pets, or his mother's ashes, even though he knew the latter had been blown to Killarney on the day they were scattered. Having such deadly material to hand made Heskyn feel strong, a Viking conqueror, standing seven feet tall, with an axe that could cleave an ox's head in half with a single smite. It was sexual, too, this feeling, made him feel manly, deadly, complete.

In front of the iron range in Mrs Flowers' kitchen Heskyn became uber-efficient, like a German, robotic car production assembly line. He cracked eggs by the dozen and hand-whisked them into an oxlip-coloured froth. He kept the bacon rashers frying by the score, keeping them warm, along with the toast, in the oven. There were cherry tomatoes, hash browns, beans and wide-brimmed Portobello mushrooms grilled so that they bubbled juice through aromatic, crinkled skins. And there were local cockles and laver bread, too, dutifully rolled in oats and fried to perfection, not to mention bright jugs of Sicilian blood oranges, freshly squeezed. As Last Breakfasts go, this was a triumph of the form.

Heskyn put on his protective mask as the doomed navvies were drinking tea and opened the first phial near the serving hatch. Whatever unclassified, or possibly unclassifiable reagent was in the phial worked like billy-o, dispatching the burly men as if they were lab mice. They clutched their throats but fell to the ground silently as whateveritwas did its thing. He screwed the lid back on the phial and walked out of the house, not taking off the mask. Heskyn looked like a beekeeper as he walked past Lidl and on to Resolven Road, taking off the mask at the corner with Clydach Close where he dropped it into a skip. He felt big, walked tall, was glad they'd all enjoyed the sumptuous, cholesterol-saturated meal.

He had had the foresight to rent a room in advance where he could lie low for a while. It was a tiny place, no bigger than a monk's cell, in a warren of rooms in a converted mental hospital, which now served as a brothel. There were prostitutes of all ages – men, women, rent boys, acrobats. Heskyn had been given the room at a peppercorn rent, on condition that he dealt with any trouble, nipped it off at the bud, as his former cell mate and bordello controller Lenny Smythe put it. Heskyn was happy to oblige, knowing he could paralyze anyone with a little puff from his throat spray.

He enjoyed getting to know the people in the place, now called the Laurels, and get a daily glimpse or two of human frailty and desire. One of the girls, Hetty, told him about the client who wanted her to feed him digestive biscuits using her toes and paid her handsomely, by the half-packet. She also told him about the war veteran, whose story, not to mention sexual difficulties, moved Heskyn to tears.

But after a few such sessions, drinking tea with Hetty, hearing about her vibrant life among the deviants, Heskyn found that he had feelings for her. He looked forward to seeing her, to watching her warm the teapot, to appreciating the way her kimono parted as she sat down, revealing a glimpse of thigh, albeit one alive with track marks. She, in turn, seemed to enjoy his company, not to mention the cakes he baked for her in the tiny kitchenette which they shared with seven others. Profiteroles, made with home-mixed Greek yoghurt and salted caramel. Mille-feuille, made of fine thin palimpsests of flavour and true to the recipe in La Varenne's seventeenth century notebook. Hetty put on weight, plumping out after seven weeks of knowing her new friend, who made no secret of having been away in gaol.

One night he asked if she would allow him to suckle her breast and she flinched from the words, as if the beseeching question mark in his voice was a hook that would flense her skin. She couldn't so much as look at him after that, feeling betrayed and profoundly let down. Even the man with the biscuits followed protocol but Heskyn had thrown away the rule book, totally overstepping the mark and then some. That night Hetty packed her small valise and headed for the docks. She knew this Lithuanian who was good for a couple of nights' shelter. He was a beater and a trafficker but he didn't ask her for a suck of milk.

The next morning Heskyn woke feeling unutterably alone. He checked Hetty's room to find her gone, without so much as a note or a hint of a goodbye. Even the teapot was gone. A mouse came in to pick at some pastry flakes even as Heskyn stood there, becalmed and stranded in the moment.

Back in his cell of a room Heskyn ate a final maple flapjack laced with light Dominican rum, then he plumply placed his lips to the little silver trumpet of poisonous material from Porton Down. The lonely man then sounded one long, searing note, chiming out human loneliness.

The note, so unexpectedly high in its pitch and so painfully sustained, blew out over the desiccated lands of no succour, before circling the planet like a plangent banshee moan, or maybe an old-fashioned police-whistle, before settling, then, into a deep and permanently troubling silence.

Some Killing on Cydweli Flats

A scarecrow wind scythed over Pinged and Llandyry and swept away towards the old washeries, over the acres of sad earth. Here they planted the vegetables in rows so straight they grew in serried ranks, a turnip army ready to march on Llanelli.

That wind. It was a dead wind. A grey wind. A wounding wind sharp enough to flail the skin off your hands. Take off your very face if you weren't careful. Leave you looking like a swede. Really.

With the sea ready to claim the flat lands of the east, eager to inundate Lincolnshire and leave the Wash awash some agents, working for powers such as Waitrose and Sainsbury's had bought up substantial tracts of land around the Gwendraeth rivers, and along the banks of other estuaries. The markets needed their vegetables. The housewife and househusband must be served. Here, in the grey loams of the Cydweli Flats, they grew the produce they desired, to be plastic-wrapped for their fresh marriages.

They grubbed up acres of sea lavender and purslane, or otherwise blitzed the saltmarshes with selective herbicides, followed by a campaign of dumping lorry loads of nitrates on the razed earth, before finally turning the soil over with ruthless machines designed to work under big skies. Then, and only then were the marshes ready for planting.

That wind. It keened over the fields of cauliflowers, sprouts and potatoes and, because this was bleak midwinter, it seemed to blow in straight from Russia, hauling chill from the Urals and rendering the Carmarthenshire earth as hard as permafrost. In the middle distance, over toward Trimsaran and Crwbin, the only remaining stand of blackthorn hereabouts – now that so many hedges had been razed or uprooted – cowered under the effect of the wind, hunchbacked by the insistent, persistent onslaught.

As the vegetable pickers drudged through the hours of backbreak work the wind seemed to mourn those who had died in the area: Victorian dockers of mangolds, coracle men with a flair for catching sewin and cockle pickers made tubercular by the gouts of rain, the endless seeping drizzle.

Today's employers didn't give the men any protective clothing, so they made do, with sou'westers and a lot of assorted rubber wear. One man even wore flippers, and not for a laugh, either. On waterlogged days the veg fields could turn into quagmires, suck at your boots like jellyfish.

Lennie Evans, one of the young men cutting turnips for a pound-an-hour-less-than-minimum-wage was thinking with every cut green head that he shouldn't be doing this. He really shouldn't be a human robot standing under sheeting rain. He had four A-levels and three fifths of a degree in medicine and the last time he'd spent this much time slicing he'd been removing a spleen with a threadwire saw in an anatomy practical. His tutor'd said his handiwork was good enough to let him practice on a live patient if he liked. But Doctor Friss was only joking. Or half-joking at least.

But things had come to a pretty underpass. His life had been completely turned around as a consequence of a foolish mistake when he spent a night, just a single night with a woman who got pregnant and it was only then that she told him that her father happened to be someone you really shouldn't mess with, which was shorthand for a dastardly criminal in the Barry Island mafia who had a penchant for designer knives and trying out carving lessons on gripped human flesh. It all led to Len having to leave town and what was worse *his parents* having to leave town and change identities to boot. After all, this was a very well-connected sociopathic gangster who really could hunt you down wherever you were cowering. But these root veg and beet fields were off his radar. Nobody in his right mind would want to live out here.

So Len was a former medical student now plucking veg from hard ground for the daily Waitrose run, in the company of half a dozen drifters and grifters. Malc the Alc, a Scot with a leathery face, whose name said it all. The Dutchman Gerbrand, never said boo to a goose but worked like a Trojan. Dave Pearce, another drop-out who'd been doing philosophy and did seem wise for his years. Then there was Mark, a sullen junkie whose life was divided equally between work and junk and Tommy, who had a wife and seven kids somewhere in the Midlands. And, finally, Trinder, a total malcontent they'd all be glad to get shot of, as he moaned more than the wind.

They all had their work cut out. Twenty thousand root vegetables, padlocked under frost-ice, which had to be wrested from the ground, trimmed, washed and then shrink-wrapped at the farm before a driver would collect them to take them down to a central distribution centre somewhere near Magor on the M4.

Twenty thousand vegetables. Not that Len had time to ponder too much about numbers. He had other things to worry about. Such as the near-dead man they'd found in one of the old aircraft hangars just a few hours ago.

They had gone there to eat lunch, in what passed for warmth, even though it was like cold storage in there. They didn't get as far as unwrapping the sandwiches.

He was dangling. The man hung in the air, his arms suspended by two lengths of rope, each as thick as naval hawser and he'd been there long enough for his hands to whiten through lack of blood flow. They looked like two white tulips, limp, slowly desiccating.

But he was alive.

The man's voice was dry, desperate, sparking tinily like radio static. In a strained voice, but in a curious accent, the man offered Len and his mates a small fortune if they could just cut him free and get him to a hospital. He gargled out a figure of twenty thousand pounds and they knew they could probably get him to go higher. Bidding for your own life – it was always a buyer's market.

It was hard for them to place the accent even though the pain-wracked face suggested he was Romanian or Bulgarian, one of the new wave of immigrants anyway. He was weak, had lost a perilous lot of blood. The ground beneath him was like a sticky blotched carpet and Lennie was horrified to see some of the red stuff adhering to his wellingtons.

They took their positions to help.

The trouble is something awful happened as they were cutting him loose, when the dour Dutch boy Gerbrand's turnip-knife slipped, went in without fuss or ado between the man's ribs and he just seemed to deflate before them, the air leaving his body as a cold mist around the mouth, matching the bated breath of the onlookers and the bystanders in the dumb show in the cold aluminium shed, watching the man leave this life without so much as a by-your-leave or proper whimper.

They had come into the hangar as free men. Now they were burdened by what they knew, witnesses or in some cases accomplices to a death, a manslaughter and the slaughtered man lay there on the ground in front of them, his eyes glazing like mackerel.

So, what happened next happened to all of them: they were all so totally, overwhelmingly *implicated*. Trinder said they were up shit creek without a paddle, and he had a point for once.

They knew they had to get rid of the body, no doubt about that, but the soil outside was completely frozen. You'd need jackhammers, or the sort of trenching drills they use when setting telegraph poles. All they had were spades and it would take them until February to cut a hole big enough for the body.

It was Len who had the idea...

The beet boiler, set up in one corner of the hangar, was a large aluminium box, big enough to accommodate a car the size of a Mini set on a plinth of old railway sleepers. The conveyor belt rattled the beets along from the processing lines, looking like misshapen bowling balls, and they would drop into the scalding water to be boiled until they were soft.

'What if we drop him in there for an hour or so? There won't be much left of him by tea-time,' suggested Lennie, pragmatically.

They conferred and after ten minutes of ghoulish debate Malc the Alc strode over to the far wall and threw the electricity switch and started to boil the water. While that happened the men stripped the clothes from the corpse – as the death mask set rigidly. They placed the clothes in a barrel which was used for burning palette tags and set them on fire, stoking the flames with anything burnable they could find in the shed, so they added piles of wrapping paper, stuff that advertised 'Two for One Deals,' 'Finest Quality,' 'Shop Early For Christmas.'

By the time they'd done that the water was beginning to steam and so they put the body on the conveyor and it started trundling him along, lifting him slowly toward the lip of the tank. There was something, well, sacred-looking about him, the rope burns like stigmata, the flaccid belly innocent as a baby's, the sense of life being unutterably over for the stranger heading for the boil.

Lenny then had his second brainwave of the day, one that would ensure their secret was safe, that there would be no weak link in the chain.

Next to the beat-up old kettle in the far corner of the hangar there were seven mugs, one for each of the gang. Lenny's proclaimed 'Welcome to LA' in day-glo letters while there were four that were giveaways from doctors' surgeries brandishing logos for 'Xanthal,' 'Nembutose' and 'Rantiril: the laxative for the discerning bowel.' Lenny always laughed when he saw that, never grew tired of its hopelessness. Then there was a plain green mug that belonged to Ger and a chipped enamel one that Malc was strangely protective of until they found out that his mother used to keep her teeth in it and thus had sentimental value. He put them all on a makeshift tray made from a cardboard box and carried them over to the crew.

He placed the tray and the mugs on the floor in a manner which was nothing less than ceremonial. The others watched him like hawks, nervous and attentive at one and the same time.

Then he picked up the first of the mugs, his own, and took it over to the boiler. He stood there for a few seconds, a priest taking stock before the sacrament, before he turned the little brass tap that allowed you to take a sample of the liquids therein. He filled the mug an eighth full and did the same with all the others.

The men looked on horrified, their faces whitewashed with horror, as if they were wearing masks in a Noh play.

Lenny handed out the mugs and then took the first supremely significant drink, downing it in one and doing his level best to make it look as if he were doing nothing more than drinking Vimto. The others held their cups as if they contained rattlesnake juice, or the blood of the unborn, or a pint of the Devil's own piss but one by one, they drank the contents down, knowing there was some well-nigh unbelievable logic in this demonic communion. Draughts to salve their conscience? Maybe not. Drinks to bind them together forever, in a pact of silence as tight as tensile steel? Perhaps.

They stood there dumb and transfixed by the moment, the taste hard to get rid of as it was more than just taste. It was a memory they couldn't excise, a portent of what prison food would taste like if they weren't careful, now that they'd entered fatefully into in a pact of silence, like so many Trappist monks.

And that might have been that. Seven workers had been bound together by an impossible guilty secret, a stain on their collective souls as bright as beetroot. Except there was a scurry in the corner of the hangar, where an outsize rat, big as a small domestic cat, slunk behind some old silage sacks. A metallic glint attracted Lennie's attention and when he looked more closely he saw a chain and that chain connected to an attaché case, like the sort of thing you'd see attached to the wrist of a diamond mule in a Bond movie. He picked up the case and put it on a straw bale to take a better look.

'You'd better put it back where you found it.' It was Gerbrand, whose voice was unfamiliar to them all, and gained some authority from that fact. Trinder said whatever it was it belonged to someone else and they were all going to die painful deaths which wasn't useful.

But curiosity needs to kill the cat.

Lennie picked up a sharp-edged tool from a pile of metal detritus and snapped open the lock with surprising ease.

They'd all seen scenes like this one in films, where the lid of a case opens up to reveal tightly-packed blocks of currency. Michael Caine's usually somewhere about, or George Clooney and there's a soundtrack that's a shimmer of violins.

They looked at it aghast before feeling the need to count it and when they unpeeled one of the blocks and found it was a major amount of money in itself, fifty pounds short of fifty thousand pounds and that fifty was probably a miscount so they realized that they had stumbled upon an honest to goodness fortune even though there was probably little that was honest behind it. Then the Dutch boy spoke again and this time his voice had the timbre of the oracle at Delphi.

'I saw a helicopter.'

They waited for amplification which came very slowly, phrase by phrase.

'It came in off the sea and landed just outside this place.'

Another pause, a long one.

'Then I saw a man with a chain attached to his wrist coming out of the helicopter and the chain was attached to the case.'

'This case?' asked Lennie, his voice a little high-pitched, a bit heliumed-up with anxiety.

'Yes. This case. This case was attached to his wrist by a length of chain. He then came out of here without it.'

Another pause, painfully long. Their eyes egged him on to continue.

'And then he ran to the helicopter, jumped on board and it took off again in the direction of the sea.'

The information bludgeoned them into silence. It was a while before they could breathe properly, let alone speak.

Lennie was the one to sum it up, the scale of their dilemma.

'So there'll be someone coming to pick it up. Maybe the dead guy was the one who came to pick it up and they tried to find out where it was hidden.'

'They?' queried Malc the Alc.

'It would take more than one person to hang a man from ropes in the air, Malcolm. That's self-evident.' Lennie was taking charge, minute by minute.

Malc looked crestfallen, his eyes puppy eyes, maybe for the first time in his life.

'So they'll be back...'

'Or maybe they haven't gone away. Maybe they're watching this place, waiting for Mr Dead's accomplice to show up,' offered Trinder almost chirpily. No wonder they all loathed him.

'Is it time for us to start shitting ourselves?' suggested Dave Pearce, at his helpful best. You could just tell he was a philosophy graduate. The way he cut to the heart of the matter. Made you think.

'I think we should take a vote,' offered Lennie, adding that by his reckoning each one of them would have at least four hundred thousand pounds before apologizing that he wasn't that good at maths. But he was near the mark, he maintained.

'Anyway,' he added, 'there's a lot of money there, and so there's a lot of money divided by seven.'

'They'll slit out throats,' said Gebrand, who was getting almost chatty.

'If they can find us,' said Malc.

'Oh, they'll find us all right,' chipped in Mark who was already imagining grade A smack that he wouldn't have to buy off the skanky dealers he normally visited in their rat holes. Opiates had made him depressive. It figures.

When it came down to it they voted to take the money and run. Or rather, hide.

And for four long days nothing happened. In fact, by the fourth day most of them had started to dream about what they'd end up doing when they weren't on the veg and their thoughts turned positively tropical, with sun-kissed beaches and pina coladas and lots of lying around and not a Brussels fucking sprout within a million miles. In their dreamy reveries they drank a lot and stayed warm all day and never had to bend over with a knife in their hands to cut a stubborn stalk ever again.

They thought these thoughts in silence, in a nervous stubborn silence, which weighed down on them as if they had breeze blocks on their shoulders.

Then on the fifth day, when they were all strung out in a long line picking cauli, they heard the drone of a far-off helicopter which then grew louder as it buzzed in low over St Ishmaels and Salmon Scar. Within minutes it was right overhead, which made them all nervous beyond, so it was with a huge sigh of relief that they watched it pass over and keep heading east although it didn't pass far enough east, but rather veered and banked and abruptly landed on the old earthwork known as the Bank O' Lords.

The doors of the helicopter opened and a dozen men in black silk suits, each man wearing a black balaclava mask, ran out. The swords they carried, or rather the scimitars they carried glistened in the late afternoon sun. The men didn't stop to appreciate the exotic spectacle, tearing the hell away across the vegetable rows, stumbling over the cut stalks which acted like trip wires, like stumbling blocks. Lennie saw the Dutch boy get beheaded even as he managed to reach a little boat tied up on the biggest creek feeding into the Gwendraeth Fawr. He saw a severed hand lying on a bed of sea purslane, the fingers clenching and unclenching uselessly before turning rigid. He saw smears of red against the purplish greens of the marsh grasses, like a painting of butchery.

Lennie managed to get its outboard engine racing and he had the forethought to leave his jacket draped over the back of the boat when he slid into the water, watching the craft head straight out to sea. And by some miracle, some ridiculous miracle, the men didn't actually see him slink into the muddy water, and by the time they saw the boat and ran back to the chopper to send it skywards to chase after the boat Lennie had managed to crawl his way into the buckthorn growth, which was a place that tore at your skin, a terrible place of savage thorns which could spear your eyeballs. But just as he felt the threat of the sharp-spined plants so too did he feel their protective safety as he pushed himself further in, knowing there were bloody acres of the stuff. Unless they had thermal imaging equipment he was safe, and the good thing was that the buckthorn groves – if you could call them that – abutted the dried up concrete culvert where they'd left the case. The whole thing almost made a religious man of him, but not quite.

Lennie still thinks of that day, not that often it has to be said because who would want to cultivate the stuff of nightmares, truth be told? To remember drinking a man's vital juices mixed with beetroot. To recall a severed hand, palping the very moments of death.

It's a warm wind that blows over the beach on Antigua and the birds are more colourful than any postage stamp. Sometimes, when he dozes like this, even as the afternoon sun turns from satsuma slowly through to pearl, the men in their bandanas run in from dark corners, across the Gwendraeth marshlands and Cydweli Flats. They give chase, vibrant with imprecations and alive with their lunging scimitars and he hears that scarecrow wind as it shivers the leaves. He may then shudder himself awake, or choose to fall into deeper sleep and leave them far behind.

One thing's for certain in his Caribbean home. He will never ever eat a root vegetable again in his life and the very words Brussels sprouts give him the hives.

For him, now, life is all papaya and he likes it that way.

Yes, all papaya and ghost crabs nibbling the flesh of his heels as he paddles in the waves: a shirr of blue water as it laps against his toes.

Yes, life is good now.

As the sun settles into the sea. And as the day's heat, blow-lamped over the mangrove line, must now surely dissipate, allowing the cooling zephyr of the night to blow right on through.

Only the Lonely

Tarry. That was his name. Not Terry but Tarry, the product of a misprint down at the registrar's which had then stuck because his parents got a lot of laughs out of it. Never tarry. Ho, ho. Hee-hee.

What made it worse was that his father's surname was Harry. Tarry grew up living in a distorting echo chamber.

So, at the age of forty three, hospital dogsbody Tarry Harry's life was cursed by his own silly, sing-song name and a living that was far from easy. He lived hand to mouth and the most he had to look forward to each day was making old people's pudenda look like firstborns as he slathered the razor round their private parts. For thirty pence an hour more than the minimum wage he prepared folk for next day's surgery, applying lashings of antiseptic soap which came from a former nerve gas distillery in Russia. It was rancid, evil stuff that evoked the sort of cheap pine after shave you bought in Poundworld that made you smell like a Christmas tree. It was a smell he couldn't get rid of. One day the sheer awfulness of the aroma made him put a scissor blade up one nostril in the hope he could make it go away. He was lucky he worked in a hospital because otherwise they might not have been able to staunch the blood in time. He almost pierced his brain. The soap smelled that bad.

So he was never going to win hands down in the dating game, that's for certain. It wasn't as if his life wasn't anything other than major crapola to begin with. Had he, say, ever found himself at one of those exquisitely chic parties where elegant creatures flit from table to table and one of those unutterably beautiful goddesses in their perfect dresses had deigned to dawdle on her high heels long enough to ask him what he did for a living he'd have had to tell her that he shaved people. With a badger hair brush. Using antiseptic soap. In the hospital. Just before operations. Undercarriages mainly.

He didn't think they'd have stayed long enough to find out his name. Which was in itself a blessing.

Oh Tarry!

But that was as nothing to what happened to him one fine Thursday in March. That afternoon it seemed as if the whole pathetic universe of his life might be entirely flushed down the shitter.

It was time for the verdict on some tests they'd performed. The doctor'd gone through the standard, almost pantomime routine. Did he want the good news first or the bad news? Tarry'd plumped for the bad news only to be told there wasn't any good news. Doctor Maggs then asked him if he was watching any boxed sets at the moment and Tarry told him he was half way through the second series of *Mad Men* and the redoubtable doctor told him what happened in the second half of the run just because Tarry wouldn't live long enough to see it. This was not the most uplifting conversation in his life.

That afternoon he went back to work with a heavy heart. He was due to help a cancer patient but the irony of being sicker than the patient on the table in front of him was not lost on Tarry.

'How's it going?' he asked the old man, who looked content for someone about to go under the knife. Mind you the consultant was a wizard with the scalpel and had taken out some growths that would have been beyond the fetch of other men.

'Not too bad, considering,' he answered.

'Been waiting long?'

'Only ten minutes.'

'No, I mean for the op. Been on the waiting list for long?'

'No, Not too long. They got me in here within, what was it, three weeks.'

'What you got wrong with you if you don't mind me asking?'

It turned out that the man had his cancer in exactly the same place as Tarry, which made him consider for a moment how he might be able to replace him in the operating theatre, jump the queue, get the whole thing over and done with this very afternoon. He could knock him out with chloroform, which was kept, after all, in the cupboard just behind him. He would then shave himself and he had every confidence in his ability to do this as this was his skill, just as other people played the violin, or gave out parking tickets. Where would he put the unconscious contented man? The broom cupboard had just enough room to place him on a chair and shut the door. But then the old man saved himself by asking Tarry a question...

'Do you think we're put on this earth for a purpose?'

Tarry tarried before answering.

'I think I was put here to see if there was any limit to loneliness.'

The old man found this a withering answer and if he hadn't been already lying down the bleakness of it would have floored him.

'Do you not have friends? Family? Colleagues?'

'I have a boss who tells me what I have to do each day. It usually takes him two sentences and he's not one for small talk. That is the extent of conversation. I live by myself. I keep myself to myself. But I dream of company, of companionship.'

'Come to tea with us, with me and the wife. When I'm out of here. Friday apparently.'

Tarry lifted the man's surgical gown and slathered some lather over his stomach.

'That would be nice. No, that would be magical. Tell me, what is your wife's name and does she like cake? I've always wanted to go to someone's house for tea and take some cake. I like Battenburg myself but apparently not everyone likes marzipan. Am I right?'

The old man didn't answer because he had dozed off. Tarry looked at him benignly, as a friend sometimes looks at a friend.

'Ready?' asked the staff nurse, popping her head around the door of surgical suite three.

'Ready as he'll ever be.'

He took in a deep breath.'

'Nurse, could I ask you be especially careful with this man. He's an old friend of mine...'

'That we'll do. And the good news is that Samuel is the anesthetist and he's never lost anyone under his care. Between him and the surgeon I think we have a dream team going here.'

They wheeled the gurney in and the red light went on above the door.

Tarry packed away his bits and pieces. Battenburg, he thought, yes, that would be his choice. And maybe some alcoholic drink or other. Rioja, he'd heard that was good. After all they would be celebrating the best of things, they would be celebrating nothing less than life itself, in all its dazzling glory.

Bowing Out

When Gruff started to get all antsy about not being able to find his violin his partner Belle didn't think too much about it. He'd only played it once during the whole crazy span of their relationship when they'd had a spirited argument about Edward Elgar.

'It's there in the music... the land is all there,' he'd blustered before storming off to the bedroom. She listened to the clattering sounds of a thirty-year old man ferreting around and swearing loudly. He emerged triumphantly, holding the battered case like a trophy.

And then, in the kitchen, he played to prove his point – that you could hear the shape of the Malvern hills in the curves of the melody. As he did so he incanted the names of places in the area, creating a little mantra. Brand Green and Ravenshill. Frith Wood and Haysland Spring. The violin music was an undertow to the names, adding to their evocation and appeal. Gruff knew the area around Malvern really well and he and Belle had walked it many times. He would always do that thing he did, which was stride a dozen paces ahead of her and then pause condescendingly near a tree or stile waiting for her to catch up. But when she did he would always kiss her, which made the slight ignominy worth it.

On those trips to the Malverns they would always stay at the same bed and breakfast run by a Mrs Vincent who had a cat fitted with a hearing aid which if not properly adjusted, Gruff reckoned, might make the patter of mice sound like gunshot. Over a full English Gruff would always surprise Belle with his local knowledge. Like the time he suggested visiting the National Michaelmas Daisy Collection. 'The National Michaelmas Daisy Collection?' she'd queried, in a voice sing-song with sarcasm. But that afternoon he took them to Picton Gardens and all the flowers were in bloom, the tended beds a subtle riot of purple and yellow.

'Told ya,' said Gruff, as he took her hand, noting some late bumblebees and leading her to some tea and scones.

The music finished and with it Belle's memories of the Malverns. 'They're all doing it,' Gruff argued, as he put away the instrument. 'Sibelius summoning up all those Finnish lakes and endless tracts of birch forest. Copeland with his Appalachian hills. You can love a place so well that it becomes a part of you. It's natural it should breach in the music, make itself apparent.'

Belle wanted to spout a list of all the composers who weren't doing it but Gruff was in one of his dogmatic moods.

'There was this critic who said of Elgar's piece that "Each time the opening phrase of melody is repeated it vanishes..."'

He nodded solemnly, as if keeping time not only with the remembered notes but also as if he was keeping time with the words, which he continued to recite...

'"In a mysterious coruscation of ascending notes which suggest the swift passing of a beauty once cherished as the hope and sum of life."'

The hope and sum of life. They had both been compressed into that moment, not to mention the 'swift passing beauty' as Gruff had played his violin with all grace and sunlight had reflected like magnesium flares from parked cars outside. At that moment she knew she couldn't love anyone more than this. Unknowingly, he had been playing the soundtrack to how she felt about him. Him and his funny ways. The man who was putting his violin away. She had heard those hills, she really had.

And that was that. Belle hadn't heard a squeak out of that instrument until now. Then he took it out of the house under his arm, as if he were ashamed of it, as if he was off to do some busking down the High Street.

One of the first things Gruff had ever told her about music was how the notes on the stave looked like swallows waiting to fly off to South Africa, to the reed-beds of the Cape. Quavers poised there on the wires, crotchets twittering with excitement.

'Because the notes do take off you know, the violin bow releases them and they take to the air. Imagine, say, the Albert Hall during the Proms, the great curved space filled with thousands of tiny birds set free by the string section. That's what it's like.'

Belle felt obliged to ask about the timpani as their notes didn't sound like swallows. They were too big and boomy for that.

'You're quite right,' said Gruff, stroking his hipster beard as if in meditation. 'The percussionists send out starlings, raucous, rowdy birds that want to fill the world with seven kinds of metallic chatter. The kettle drums however are bitterns, making the sound of foghorns in the fens.'

Gruff was always doing that. Saying things that were bonkers and beautiful at the same time.

He and his violin didn't return for hours and by the time he did Belle had already eaten and put away the plates. Gruff looked exhausted and didn't have enough pep to answer her questions. Where had he been? What had he been up to?

He had finished slurping up his miso soup when the phone rang. It was Trevor, Belle's half brother asking if Gruff was OK because someone had seen him playing the violin in the park, near the pond where the little boy drowned. He'd been standing there near the little pile of floral tributes apparently, and had drawn quite a crowd. Gruff had made a lot of them cry, the piece he'd been playing full of primal sadness.

'That was Trev,' Belle volunteered, as she switched off her phone. ' Said he'd heard about your impromptu open air concert. Said you were brilliant.'

'Wrong. Samuel Barber was brilliant. He was the one who wrote the *Adagio for Strings*. All I did was deliver the melody. It's as sad as Sundays.'

'May I ask why?'

'It was the anniversary of the boy's death and I reckoned the parents would be there. I wanted to play for them. And they were there. And when they started to cry they started everyone else off, egged on by the effect of the minor scale. It was all caterwauling grief down at the pond side, I can tell you. It's powerful stuff, Barber's tune, his "melody like the hesitant climbing of stairs," as someone once put it. It takes you somewhere you may not want to go. But when you get there you realize it's the only place you really need to be. Takes you to the very heart of grief.'

'What made you do this?' Belle asked him, almost suspiciously. It was so out of character. Normally he was shy, avoided people's gaze on the bus or in the pub, steered clear of crowds, even to the point of his behaviour resembling a psychological kink.

Wordlessly Gruff put on a YouTube clip. It showed a young man playing a cello. The plangent music, despite its coming from the laptop speaker, seemed to fill every corner of the living room. She found it hard to breathe because of its bare emotion.

'His name is Vedran Smailović. Twenty two people had been killed while queuing for bread in the market in Sarajevo. This guy turned up every day for twenty two days performing things like Albinoni's *Adagio in G Minor*.'

They watched this young man with his outsize handlebar

moustache and crumpled tuxedo playing amongst the rubble of his shattered city, his head held high despite the threat of sniper fire. Sarajevo was in the middle of a brutal siege, Gruff explained, and yet this man, Vedran Smailović was bestowing some sort of freedom. The freedom for a besieged city to express its grief, to ascend the scales of suffering.

'The music was a conduit for people's pain. And a sort of benediction. I thought I'd do the same. At People's Park.'

That might have been that were it not for clips of Gruff playing appearing online and then the local newspaper got wind of it and sent round a reporter who'd been tipped off by Trev who played snooker with him. After the article appeared Gruff started to get requests to play in funerals like Smailović did in the Balkans but he turned them all down, telling people they could get good recordings of all of the music to play in church or in the crematorium and even recommending artists or re-masterings he particularly liked.

Then one day he got a call from someone in Brighton. A young girl, an art student called Catriona, who apologised for tracking him down. Gruff immediately suspected Trev, who was a bit cavalier when it came to handing out Gruff's personal details.

'I'd like to invite you to come play with us. There was this house fire you see and me and my mate Carl thought we'd follow your example and play something on the day of the funeral. And then Carl suggested asking whether you'd like to join us.'

There was a long, velveteen silence before the young woman started speaking again.

'A whole family died. Parents, five children. Only one son survived, so I guess we're playing for him. And for any extended family who show up...'

Gruff had made up his mind but felt obliged to ask one thing first. Which instruments did Catriona and Carl play?

Catriona played viola, so that was OK but Carl was a drummer, which seemed a little bit problematical.

Sensing his scepticism Catriona said that he'd be using just one drum and a set of brushes, playing them softly like Buddy Rich. He could play really quietly, she said. He could make the sound of a mist rising from a river valley, he really could. It was reassurance enough.

'Right, I'll do it. I'll come down the night before so we can practise. I'll text you the time of train I'll be coming in on.'

The three of them arrived at the crematorium well ahead of time and had a word with the vicar, who luckily was an enlightened fellow and could see the point in what they were suggesting. In fact he took it in his stride in a way that not one of them was expecting. The Reverend Smith even volunteered to have a word with the mourners, to make sure they understood what the unexpected visitors were about. Then they all stood as a group to ponder the meaning of the sad array of trestle tables that had been set up next to the lectern, to take the extra coffins.

The vicar hadn't officiated at a job-lot funeral before and sincerely hoped he wouldn't have to again. Having this trio of musicians turn up was in keeping somehow with the distressingly sad nature of the occasion. It tested his sense of a personal God. Why so much suffering? he asked himself. Why not have some music?

The service was brief, almost perfunctory, in part because the people who needed to hear good things being said about the family were the family members themselves and they were dead.

Gruff had chosen Massenet's *Meditation* and he and Catriona had practised it a dozen times, with him improvising in a dozen places even as Carl added a quiet military beat, entirely in keeping with a funeral, a processional series of rimshots leading to deft and subtle work with the brushes.

They had each dressed in black in the morning, even though Catriona added a twist of red scarf in defiance of the impending gloom and solemnity. Gruff was in casual black, jeans and a jacket while Carl wore a black T-shirt which he'd ironed for the first time, out of respect.

It was quite a gathering with news crews filming the mourners as they arrived, trying to be discrete but failing comprehensively as men with heavy duty Sony cameras tend to do when trying to blend in.

At the end of the service, the vicar pressed the button to close the curtain around the processional arrangement of caskets.

The three of them strode forward and played on a nod.

The music was a river of grief flowing black and treacly and there was hardly a soul among them who was not touched by its slow majesty. They remembered loved ones plucked like flowers in mid bloom and parents scythed from the earth by the reaper's punctilious sweeping. And Gruff found something new within himself as he applied lacquers of meaning to the music, much as age had added darker layers to his instrument. Mahogany textures, a resinous wash to the music.

He was handling the violin now with all tenderness, as if dandling a new born baby in a swaddling of cloth.

Meanwhile Carl was locked in his tempo, a human metronome, imagining himself to be a member of Radiohead, that sort of precise percussionist. Catriona was entirely lost, on some astral plane, cut loose from herself. She stood on a piece of drifting glacier, the cold world surrounding her made even colder by the piece she played, as she cut the bind, unloosed herself from the work of a nineteenth century composer and played her own soul's tune.

And this, this trio's *tightening* was the stuff of transfiguration, the three's released birds of sound and tapped notes and calibrated glissandi giving pause, making the congregation think again about their lives. To ponder what this terrible accident – this house fire which turned a family into charred cinder sculptures – meant in the greater scheme of things. And there was wailing now, the congregation morphing into keeners, their desperate wails broken up only by the need to take in great draughts of oxygen, even as Gruff 's violin egged them ever on and on, onto the desolate plains. It was almost too much, and then the trio took them further, ascending the great mountain of all human loss. Yes, three people were able to do this by playing from within themselves and recognising the suffering all around them, channelling it into the chatter of mixed flocks of birds, now rooks and jackdaws and sub-sonic raven croaks – blackening sounds that could blot out the sun.

As they started their last section a fifteen year old boy got up from the front row of the congregation and joined them, fishing out a tin whistle from his jacket pocket. He was the sole surviving member of the family and played only a small range of notes but played them with a deep sincerity, silver darts of sound piercing the collective hearts of all inside.

What he played exactly was a matter of some disagreement. Later that morning, people threading down the long path between poplars leading away from the crematorium debated among themselves. Some thought it an Irish thing, like a reel but others countered that you could dance to a reel and you'd have to be on crutches to be able to dance to that thin tune. Others thought it was a hobo song, something sung on the great iron horse crossing America, but when pressed to name the song they would fall silent, thinking only of the whistling wind through the telegraph wires. Only the boy knew what it was and he needed to keep that a secret, as it was a tune his family loved and he didn't want to give too much away.

As he played it he could hear his mother whistling the tune at his bedside when he was at that age when he could start to remember things, five or six years old maybe and in that whistle was the warmth and strength and sure-fire sense of musicality of the woman who'd gone up in flames. *Incinderated* as he put it, creating a new word to include in the lexicon of hurt. Never to whistle again in this life. That was for certain. When he finished playing applause erupted like firecrackers and even the vicar joined in.

The young lad, whose name was Luke, stuck with Gruff, Cat and Carl after the service, told them about the past weeks. He'd had counselling and a GP had prescribed purple pills which were nothing short of knock out drops but the absence, the withering absence of his mother, father, brothers, sister was too much to bear. Too much to even begin to imagine a place and a time when it would be bearable. His eyes were lagoons of worry. Catriona gave him some of the usual platitudes... about time being a healer and how he should live his life more fully now, and carry memories of his family with him as he did so, an enduring and portable memorial yet the sadness in his eyes was palpable, glacial.

All this while Luke held his whistle tightly, as if it were all that was left of an umbilical.

Someone in the congregation that day, probably more than one person, posted a clip of the performance online and it took less time than did a Justin Bieber song to become totally viral, people downloading it by the thousand, choosing it as a favourite by the million, so many people affected by it. It was the full and revealing expression of the zeitgeist.

By the time Gruff returned home he had had to grow used to staring looks from strangers on the train. He got off the train only to be assaulted by a group of teenage girls who wanted to touch his clothes. The caterwauling of the seven or eight girls who milled around Gruff attracted the attention of two community support officers who walked towards them not knowing if they needed autograph books or Tasers. Even they'd worked out who he was.

Back home Bella was a little cowed by his presence. He was not the same man whose cheek she had kissed before he left for the South. He was famous now and his gift for allowing folk to feel their pain and then relinquish it, had gone viral. More than that – gone viral at the fastest rate of any film or meme or scurrilous joke that had ever graced or disgraced social media. It had been e-mailed by a million users, clicked onward into the ether-space by a sub-continent's worth of users, all moved beyond consolation by the music and the young man's intervention on the whistle and the way in which he'd changed the mood. Yes, that was the thing. The way he'd changed the mood of things, exchanged the sober, sombre tone for an upbeat moment, his little tune some sort of clarion call.

Gruff was settling down to read some poetry in the bath to take his mind off things when Belle came in carrying the TV with its electrical lead at full stretch.

'Ah, the perfect murder,' said Gruff. '"He was watching the TV from the comfort of his own bath when the set accidentally dropped into the suds, electrocuting him totally," said his common law wife Belle at the inquest.'

'Don't be a tool,' said Belle, placing the set on the little cupboard. 'This is the *Ten O' Clock News* and you're on it. Coming up next they said.'

And with that the announcer cued a news item about the song that had taken the UK by storm suggesting it was tipped to be next week's number one hit.

'But we haven't recorded it...'

'Hush. We'll talk about that later... a man from Warner Brothers rang earlier today...'

The news item featured a few clips of the song interspersed with interviews with experts on internet usage talking about mega surge and hyper promotion. It was akin to the death of Diana, said an earnest looking man from the University of Warwick who stood there in a Harris tweed jacket a size too big.

And then they played a longer clip to round off the item and when the camera cut back to the studio the presenter was crying.

'Heck, Huw Edwards is weeping,' said Gruff, at last astonished by the sequence of events. 'He's a tough cookie. Doesn't get worked up in war zones and look at him now, blubbering like a baby.'

At that the veteran broadcaster managed to pull himself together, even as a disembodied hand reached in from the left of frame and handed him a paper tissue.

'There'll be more on this story in a special edition of *Newsnight* which follows this programme over on BBC2.'

'*Newsnight*,' said Gruff. 'About us. I'll have to watch that.' A moment later one of the producers from current affairs was on the phone, coaxing him into doing a Skype interview at ten to eleven.

So Belle was able to watch her partner on TV from the room next door and it really was a special edition, the whole programme devoted to it, even though the news, if it really was news was still breaking.

Gruff was articulate and erudite and after his contribution he sat down to watch the end of the show. It was the usual format. The presenter sat on one side and three well groomed contributors sat opposite. They talked about broken Britain, a people forlorn, the sundering of Europe.

It was the woman on the end of the panel who stole the show in Gruff's opinion, making an explicit reference to Vedran Smailović, the cellist of Sarajevo. This made Gruff sit up straight and as if that wasn't enough they then had a live feed from Smailović's house in Northern Ireland and the man himself was interviewed, his voice now tinged with a peaty brogue. The cellist suggested that the country, the whole of the UK was so bruised after leaving Europe and the economic and social consequences that had followed like a wrecking ball. People needed healing, he maintained, no they craved healing with all their hearts. These musicians were the means to do just that, and were a conduit for all the pain that was swilling around, making bitter people more bitter and hurt ones more hurt.

And then the killer line...

'I should like to play with them. I should like to bring my cello out of retirement.'

With that the presenter had to close the show and as Belle switched off the telly Gruff seemed to dissolve on the sofa.

'He wants to play with us,' said Gruff in a quavering voice that belonged to a man who had been transported. He was no longer in a flat in Harrogate but was, rather, in the middle of his favourite painting, *The Plains of Heaven* by John Martin where feathered droves of angels commanded the middle ground against a backdrop of celestial mountains, their peaks glowing like snow lamps. He was that happy. 'He wants to play with us,' he repeated, to enjoy the words.

It was a glorious moment. In his mind's eye he could survey the very fields of heaven and hear a sonorous cello playing as a soundtrack. Gruff knew he'd set off something big here, something seemingly out of his control.

With that the doorbell sounded and Gruff warned Belle that if it was the paparazzi she should let them have it with some burning tar, pour it over them from the balcony.

'An Englishman's home is his castle and all that.'

But when she looked through the visitor camera she could see a young lad standing there. The one who'd been on telly and everywhere else these past ten hours. Luke.

The three of them sat in the living room sipping hot chocolate and not saying very much. The adults were stunned by the sheer momentum of what was happening, such that they had had to switch off both their phones to stop them ringing all the time while the young lad, battered by grief before all this happened now looked as if he couldn't focus on the thumb he was sucking from time to time.

'Thank you for the drink,' he said after a while.

'Cocoa, from Madagascar,' said Belle helpfully, or at least managing to fill in some of the awkwardness by sharing this sweet nugget of fact.

'We were just watching *us* on TV,' volunteered Gruff, almost too chirpily considering this young man was the poster boy for pain.

'And we had a volunteer to come join us.'

'I thought I'd play just once, just the once. It felt right at the time.'

'You might have to do it twice. People seem to need us, we have something they want, that helps them somehow.'

The three sipped their cocoa, lost in thought before making up a bed for their young visitor.

Later in bed Belle turned to Gruff and asked in a hushed whisper if Luke would be all right.

'He'll be fine. He's with us now. We'll take care of him.'

And Belle had no objections at all to this most casual of adoptions.

The next few days were a whirlwind of activity, the flat under siege from newspapermen and TV crews. They tried all manner of strategies – above board and underhand – to get the scoop, the lowdown, the world exclusive. When Belle ordered takeaway food it was delivered by a fake delivery boy and Belle only just managed to rumble him in time when she remembered that she had ordered Chinese food not pizza. There were cash offers made and at one point a business card belonging to the London correspondent of ABC was pushed through the door asking if they could possibly make themselves available to be interviewed by Michelle Obama for their peak-time show *Sixty Minutes*.

'This is beyond ridiculous,' said Belle as she served up some hot and sour soup.

'These sesame prawns are fantastic,' said Gruff who was trying to be blasé after being photographed from a dozen angles as he took in the food. There was even a photographer hanging from the balcony upstairs using one arm like an orangutan, taking a snap with little regard for his own life.

'We'll have to move if this carries on,' said Belle.

'We'll have to change our names,' suggested Gruff through a mouthful of seaweed. 'Like in a witness protection programme.'

'And what about Michelle?'

'Oh so we're on first name terms with the First Lady are we now?'

'We'd better ask Luke.'

Luke had slept for a straight eighteen hours and was looking new-born. His hair had been combed for the first time in weeks and the first thing he did when he sat down with them at the kitchen table was take Belle's hand and squeeze it before saying 'Thank you' with an earnestness that was quite disarming.

'There's no need,' said Belle, holding back the tears. The young man was an angel, come to live among them. Gruff looked at him with all the regard of a proud father who has seen his son score a winning rugby try.

'So what would the man whose music makes the steeliest TV presenter break down like for brunch. We have eggs.'

'Eggs with my family,' said Luke which set off the waterworks in Belle, who retired to another room to weep disconsolately.

'I didn't mean to do that,' he apologised.

'There's a lot of stuff you didn't mean to do. Like throw out a lifeline to broken Britain, but you did and all I can say is that I was glad I was there when you did. Do you know people are seriously discussing changing the national anthem...'

'What, for my little tune?'

'Yes, your little tune, coupled with my fine playing and Cat's viola and Carl on drums. Don't forget us,' said Gruff, ribbing the 'Whistling Genius' as he'd been dubbed by the *Mail*. He had a copy in front of him, Luke's face pixillated from being blown up large.

'This is not a time for forgetting,' said Luke, and the serious tone in his voice sounded like a reprimand to Gruff's ears, remembering that Luke's defiant, silvery melody flew in the face of the boy's misery.

But Gruff knew what to say.

'Do you want to live here? You can stay as long as you like.'

'But will they go away?' he asked, nodding in the direction of the media scrum outside. They were now a fully-fledged encampment and had starting running cables from neighbours' electricity sockets, ordered in coffee urns, sun parasols and rain umbrellas, covering all bases.

'Oh yes, the press pack always moves on to hunt elsewhere. Novelty is like fresh blood for them. They need the shock of the new like some people need heroin.'

'Oh but when they hear about this little offer they'll be buying the flats either side of us,' said Gruff ,who was reading yet another extraordinary e-mail that had just come in.

'Dear Gruff Holmes,' it read. 'I am writing on behalf of the Archbishop of York...'

'Does he know you're a pagan?' piped up Belle from the kitchen, laughing.

'... To ask whether you and your talented friends might consider performing at a concert at York Minster Cathedral. We are organising a "Concert of Hope" and the spiritual uplift provided by your song seems to be just the very thing to conclude our evening. We do not have a specific date in mind but are thinking about the end of the month. I should tell you that we already have the support of broadcasters and one of the major newspapers, not least because we have secured the services of Daniel Barenboim and his West-

Eastern Divan Orchestra, which as you probably know is made up of young musicians from countries such as Israel and Palestine. I have taken the liberty of contacting Mr Barenboim and he has indicated that his players would be happy to accompany you should you wish...'

'This is nuts,' said Gruff.

'Double nuts,' said Luke, who had no idea what a York Minster was, nor, for that matter, what an archbishop was. But he could see this was a big deal as Gruff was re-reading the e-mail carefully, mouthing some of the words as he did so.

Belle came in with a plate of freshly made chocolate cookies.

'I made these. Celebratory they are, now that you're going global.'

And with that Luke smiled for the first time since the fire, and it was enough to light up the room and the streets beyond, despite the grey mugginess of the day.

The concert was arranged for the last Friday of the month. The orchestra arrived from the Middle East the day before and Gruff and the others were asked in advance for their input about the order of events. So Gruff asked if Huw Edwards could be the master of ceremonies as he'd been one of the main engines of the phenomenon, as clips of him in tears had gone viral and mutated with the virus of their song to create a social network epidemic.

What was it about this little tune, this innocuous ditty, Gruff found himself asking himself, much as millions of people asked themselves the self-same question. Was it simply that a young man who had faced so much adversity and that so very recently could spirit up a jaunty tune as if he was laughing in the face of death, searching out the one bright chink of hope in the dark tunnel of bitter experience? It might just be unexplainable and one should simply leave it at that, a thing that just happened, like a comet passing through.

The Archbishop opened the evening, which was being broadcast live to a global audience bigger than the number of people who watched Live Aid. An awful lot of them didn't really understand why they would watch classical music, and listen to a religious dude from Uganda telling them what's what before listening to that song. But there they all were, in council flats and hotel rooms, in pub snugs and bingo halls, in bedsits, supermarkets, nursing homes across the land, all whistling with anticipation as they all knew the tune. It was burned into the cortices of their brains. Even the old people with dementia knew this one, could whistle it through their dentures. It was a tune that stuck.

The Archbishop read from the book of Nehemiah, Chapter 8: Verse 10. 'Do not grieve,' he said, 'for the joy of the Lord is your strength.' And then he read a poem by Dylan Thomas and the string section of the orchestra played as an undertow to the lilt of the poem and then the full orchestra walked out into the great nave of the Minster. They played some Gorecki and for some members of the TV audience it was moving beyond. And then the cellist of Sarajevo joined the young musicians, the 100 young Arabs and Jews as they play the *Adagio* and you could have cut down the footage to make the best ever advert for paper handkerchiefs, as the entire audience was weeping by this stage, the music taking them to a place of redemption, a place of understanding, where sadness faded. They were trying to heal the wounds of a country that was bleeding into insignificance. They needed art in the same way some people needed a hospital.

In the changing room the headline act was getting ready. Luke and Gruff hadn't seen the others since the whole media rollercoaster had started to pick up speed and when they exchanged notes it was hard to imagine what their lives had been like before. Hollywood offers, cheque-book journalism, all this because of a piece of music. It was triple nuts, quadruple nuts. It was quintuple nuts when the cellist came over to introduce himself and Gruff had to explain that much of this was down to him, as he told the musician about the concert for the drowned boy down at People's Park. That was only three weeks ago. It was hard to believe.

They linked hands to walk out to perform, each musician holding his or her instrument awkwardly in order to do so.

'Standby' said the TV multi-cam director as they started the predetermined sequence of which camera did what and when. The satellite feed was being picked up by no fewer than eighty countries, the majority of those still reeling from what had seemed like the greatest act of national self harm since records began. The old European flags outside the Minster flapped in a gentle breeze and not without irony. Many people couldn't say the word Brexit without it tasting like arsenic on their lips. Division begat more division. City streets fired and burned.

The musicians went to the source, to the wellspring of the deepest, simplest emotion, with Luke starting this time and the others repeating the purity of the melody like a canon. Just twenty notes or so, but notes of sweet integrity, ascending very much as the heart soars on finding love, or keeping love.

Soon each of the musicians had conjured a stream of sound into being, flowing, comingling, one coming together with the other, finding harmony where there was dissent. Gruff would have been hard pressed to tell whether he was hearing the music of the spheres or the joy of the Lord as he wove in motifs from Elgar that encouraged a tickertape of daisy petals to drift through the nave and Catriona's viola turned into a veritable jazz instrument, riffing plangently on the central theme. Carl started tapping a martial beat, onward, onward, marching unto glory which at first surprised the others until they too managed to get in step. And the cellist from Sarajevo drew out notes from the earth, sonorous sounds from the planet's mantle.

In the front pew Belle would not have been surprised if Luke had sprouted angel wings and flapped away like some outsize white vulture, gaining height over the clerestory and the ornate marquetry of the medieval rood screen. And carried on soaring, until the roof dissolved to give him access to all the celestial acres, all the gleaming fields of heaven, arcing above the earth.

But as it was the young man simply stood there, noodling his tune on a whistle that had cost him sixty pence. The others brought their music to a close, leaving just him playing, this young man called Luke, his name so appropriate for this high church setting.

He blew out one gusty final note, which had the duration of a breath and shaped within it the sheer gift of life and oxygen and hope, yes that was there, all in a shiny, silvery toot. Standing next to him Gruff could picture something in the sound.

A burble of stream. A flick of trout.

Gruff turned toward Luke with pride as he pushed him forward to take the applause.

One young man, his whistle in hand, standing in the refracted light of the Great East Window, who made the sound the light itself might make.

One young man who had produced a tiny kernel of hope.

A kernel made of music.

To plant in sad hearts.

In the hearts of those who cared sufficiently to listen.

Acknowledgements and Thanks

'Some Killings on Cydweli Flats' first appeared in *Wales Arts Review* and subsequently in book form in *A Fiction Map of Wales*, edited by John Lavin and published by the H'mm Foundation. 'Class Ghost' was first published in *Horla*. The spectral butler who prowls the lower reaches of 'The Murenger' was created for *Mysterious Maud's Chambers of Fantastical Truth*, a collaborative theatre piece devised and directed by Caroline Sabin, first performed at Insole Court, Cardiff in October 2018. 'Heskyn at Large' was part of *Wales Arts Review's* Story: Retold series, published in association with the Rhys Davies Trust. It is inspired by the Rhys Davies short story, 'Boy with a Trumpet.' 'Candles' was also published by *Wales Arts Review* for a Halloween special in 2014.

Huge thanks to Three Impostors – being David Osmond, Richard Frame and Mark Lawson-Jones – for bringing out this volume in time for it to be a sort of sixtieth birthday gift, in the hope it feels like that to the reader too. Despite the masquerade of the name Three Impostors is the sort of publisher a writer dreams of.

Any book is always a collaboration, of course and this one would be a dowdier affair without the superb cover and chapter art by S Mark Gubb and the ever dependable design skills of Andy Dark and Tomos Osmond who did the lay-out.

The Murenger, as the most convivial hostelry I know, is enshrined in the title of this volume but special thanks to Rob and Julie for creating a literate, welcoming haven, a sort of escape pod for when the world goes mad.

Diolch o galon i chi gyd.

For more books from Three Impostors please visit

www.threeimpostors.co.uk